HIS CURVY BEAUTY, BOOKS 1-3

A BBW ROMANCE COLLECTION

CURVY COLLECTIONS
BOOK ONE

LANA LOVE

LOVE HEART BOOKS

Copyright © 2019 by Lana Love

All rights reserved.

No part of this book may be reproduced in any form or by any electronic or mechanical means, including information storage and retrieval systems, without written permission from the author, except for the use of brief quotations in a book review.

❦ Created with Vellum

PROTECTING HER CURVES

TAMMY

"*L*uke, I'll be fine. I swear!" I sigh loudly, my phone wedged between my ear and my shoulder as I finish ringing up a customer. "Thanks, Mr. Jones. You can pick up your arrangement on Thursday. Your wife is going to love it!"

Mr. Jones smiles and the bell over the front door to my flower store jingles.

"Tammy," my brother Luke says, concern and frustration heavy in his voice. I wipe my hands on my apron, then grab the phone and hold it properly so that I don't get a kink in my neck. "I know you think you're safe and I know you can defend yourself."

"But…" I interrupt. "I know there's a *but* coming."

Luke's voice is muffled as he covers up his phone and responds to someone. This is something I've gotten used to, since he joined the Army. He's not supposed to talk about what he's doing and usually doesn't even tell me which country he's in.

"Tammy, the neighborhood isn't good right now. You must know what I'm talking about. I know you've been gone for a few years, with school and work. Things haven't been great – not that they ever were – and I'm worried about you. I haven't forgotten that you said that Parker's bodega was held up last week."

"Luke," I say, my amusement at his brotherly concern venturing into the territory of frustration-fueled anger. "It's not like you're here to walk me home. Who is going to come after me? I opened a flower store. Do you think people are going to steal flowers?"

Luke's laugh is a bark and I can tell he's smirking. I walk to the back of the store and check to make sure everything is set up for the morning. There is a big order for ten centerpieces and I doublecheck my order book to make sure everything I'll need will be delivered in the morning. When I'm satisfied that I haven't forgotten anything, I switch the phone to my hand and keep rubbing my neck with my other hand as I walk back to the front of the store.

"That may be true, but that doesn't mean I don't know people. Sullivan is on his way over. He's on extended leave. And I trust him with my life, which means I trust him with yours. You know him."

I gulp and my heart thumps in my chest. Hard. "Johnny Sullivan?"

"The one and only. Look, I know you haven't seen him in years. He'll make sure you get home safe and he'll help you out if you need it. Until they catch the assholes terrorizing the neighborhood, you need someone to look out for you. Until I'm back, that's Sullivan."

"Goddammit, Luke. If you weren't wherever you are, I'd smack you. I'm not some delicate flower that can't hold my own and you know it. *You're* the one who taught me how to fight and defend myself. Or have you forgotten?"

Luke exhales slowly, in the way I know he does when he's at the end of his rope with me. "Tammy. These assholes have guns and knives. I didn't teach you how to deal with that. I taught you how to deal with generic assholes who bother you at school or in a bar. I wish you'd trust me."

"Look, I gotta go," I say when I hear the bell over the door. "A customer just walked in."

"I just want you to be safe, Tammy. That's all. We're the only family that we have left. You know that I couldn't bear to have anything happen to you."

The tone of Luke's voice is softer now, and it reminds me of just how much he loves me and how much I love my brother. Sometimes I wish I didn't have him standing over my shoulder and looking out for me, but deep down, I'm glad that he does.

"I love you, too. I'll email you when I get home." I may not be able to call him reliably, but email we can do.

"You do that. And be nice to Sullivan."

I roll my eyes and smile as we end the phone call and I slide my phone into the back pocket of my jeans.

"Sorry to keep you wai…" My voice freezes in my throat. It's not another customer.

It's Johnny Sullivan. All six-foot-four of him and he's built like a shit house. I haven't seen him since I was in high school, but he's rippling with muscles and his dark hair is buzzed short. I instantly recognize him, but there's an air about him that I don't recognize. Standing in front of me, he exudes an air of power and authority. Even though I know I don't need him, he looks exactly the kind of person I'd want to have at my side if something *did* happen.

"Tammy. Hi. Been a while." Johnny shifts his weight between his feet, almost as if he's nervous.

"Hey, Johnny. I was just talking to my brother. He told me you'd show up." I busy myself making sure all the coolers are closed and that everything is put away properly. Having my own store is still so new and such a novelty, and I never get tired of touching everything and making sure that everything is exactly the way that I wanted to be.

Johnny's eyes tighten a little bit, but his gaze never wavers from me.

"I've got orders." There is a hint of a laugh in his voice, as if he also questions my need for protection.

I finish checking everything and turn to face Johnny again. He hasn't moved. Conflicting desires race through my body. Johnny was the boy I always fantasized about in high school. He ran with a rough crowd and got into a fair amount of trouble. Rumor had it that the sheriff made a deal with Johnny's father, saying that he would drop charges that would have put Johnny in prison, if Johnny agreed to join the military.

"You're not going to let me go alone, are you?" I put my hands on the counter and lean forward as I look at him. His jaw tightens and it sends ripples of desire through my body. Seeing him in front of me conjures up all of my teenage fantasies. My brother always warned me about him, saying that he was dangerous and no good for me, but that only ever made me want Johnny even more.

"That would be correct. Do you have much more to do?"

"No, I'm finished. Let's get going. We might as well get it over with as quick as possible."

A look flashes across his eyes so quickly that I question if I really saw it. We walk out the front door and I look behind me, smiling as I look at my store. *This is mine. This is my dream come true.*

Johnny matches my pace, which is considerate given that he is nearly a foot taller than I am. In the distance, there is the familiar sound of a dog barking and of cars screaming down the street.

"Sounds like drag racing," I say, tightening my scarf around my neck. Even though it's early October, the weather is colder than normal and I haven't adjusted yet.

"You would be right," Johnny says, turning his head and looking up and down the street around us. Watching him is like watching a bodyguard in a movie – his eyes roam up and down the street, watchful and protective.

"There's nobody around, but us," I tease. "Every sane person is indoors, with the heat on. Anyway, why don't you tell me what you've been up to. It's been years since I've seen you."

Johnny glances at me and his dark eyes flash. His face is hard to read and he's barely said anything except terse responses. It's starting to get frustrating.

"There's not that much to tell. I got in trouble in high school, and the Army was the solution. It's worked out okay. I've become a better man."

I stumble on a piece of uneven pavement and Johnny reaches out and steadies me, as if I weighed nothing. It's impressive, because I'm so far from weighing nothing that it's not even funny.

The warm strength of his hand on my arm fuels desire and in an instant, I'm imagining his hands underneath my clothes, caressing my bare skin and touching me in ways that would make my brother blow a fuse. When my cheeks burn with a blush, I look away from him, scared that he can read my thoughts.

"Oh… Thanks."

His hand stays on my arm slightly longer than necessary, but he doesn't say anything. We resume walking and a different kind of awkward passes between us. He keeps scanning the streets in a methodical way.

We turn the corner and stop in front of my building. I find myself wishing that we could keep walking – walking somewhere that didn't require constant vigilance.

"Same time, tomorrow?" Johnny's intense eyes bore into me and challenge me. I don't want a chaperone and he knows it.

"I really don't need to be walked home," I counter, a fresh wave of frustration bubbling up in me. But the look in Johnny's dark eyes is unwavering. The prospect of spending more time with him is appealing, though my ideas about that definitely do not include chaperoning me. Not that anything will ever happen because he's my brother's best friend and why would he even look at me?

Johnny continues to stare at me. A muscle in his jaw twitches, but he keeps waiting for me to respond.

"Fine. Same time tomorrow." I hate that I cave so quickly to him, but the truth is I can't wait until tomorrow.

JOHNNY

I watch and wait until Tammy is safely inside her building. As I start walking home, I feel like a total fool. Tammy. The girl I've wanted to talk to one-on-one, for years. What happens when I have the chance? I can barely talk in single sentences.

Seeing Tammy is like traveling back to when we were all in high school, and her brother threatening me that if I so much as touched a hair on her head, much less actually spoke to her alone, that he would kill me in creative ways that had not yet even been invented. That may be the past, but Luke's warnings still echo in my mind.

Hurting her is something I can never do. I want to protect her and love her, and never go years between seeing her again. Fuck. I don't want to even wait twenty-four hours to see her again.

The sound of metal on metal and sharp laughter immediately catches my attention. I stop walking and look around, bristling to identify what's happening. Half of the lights on the street are burnt out or broken, which means there are shadows everywhere and plenty of places for people to hide. I shake out my arms, instinctively preparing for a fight.

At the end of the block, three young men walk toward me, their pace slow and full of swagger, like they feel they own the block, if not the entire city. I know their type immediately, because I used to be that type. I used to think that working a regular job or having a regular family was a worse prison than a prison with bars. I fought against the normal life so hard, until one day I went too far and it bit me in the ass. Joining the Army literally saved my life, by teaching me the discipline, skill, and responsibility that had been lacking in my life.

"Out of the way old man," one of the boys yells at me, then guffaws in laughter.

I look at the boys more closely, assessing whether or not they are true threats or just young boys playing at being tough. I ignore them and keep on walking.

"Yeah, old man knows what's good for him." One of the boys calls out.

My muscles tense, even though I do not want to engage. They are absolutely not a threat, but if I let myself give in to any asshole trying to bait me, then not even the Army could save me from prison this time. I may have learned to control and channel my anger into something useful, but my anger never leaves me and boys like them push all the buttons that got me in trouble in high school.

I let my mind wander back to Tammy and I feel the warmth spread through my body. When Luke called and asked me to look out for her, I knew it would be awkward to see her. Not that he would know, because I sure as hell never told him how much I wanted his sister back in high school. The day we met, Luke laid down the ground rules that she was indisputably off limits. I understand he was looking out for his little sister, but I knew from the moment I saw her that she was the one and that no other woman would ever compare to her. And no woman has.

I shove my hands deep into my jacket pockets, speeding up my pace in an effort to ward off the chill of the night air.

I know Tammy is off limits…but seeing her tonight ignited emotions in me that make me realize that I've never stopped wanting her.

Once I get home, I send Luke a terse email. *Tammy's fine, and she safe at home. I'm meeting her tomorrow, too. Stay safe, brother.*

The apartment I'm renting is a generic one-bedroom, furnished with worn, old furniture. I don't have anything and don't need much, so it's perfect until I figure out my new life. After my last two tours, I had to take a break. Being a sniper is emotionally taxing for anyone who still has a conscience. Sure, some of it is reconnaissance, but that's not the part that wears you down. I'm not so far gone that I truly enjoy what I do, though I have pride that it's something I do well.

I don't know if this is where I'm going to end up or spend even another six months of my life, but coming here was an easy decision. It's a city I know and I still have a few buddies here and there. I knew Tammy was here, from Luke, though I never imagined our paths would cross so soon. I had hoped to see her, but I never thought it would be like this.

But Tammy is off limits. I know she's the one, but Luke will kill me if I touch her. She doesn't know what I did in the Army, and telling her that I'm a sniper isn't something most civilians are comfortable with.

I step into the shower and hot water sluices over my body, instantly relaxing my muscles, but it doesn't fully ease the tension that's haunted me since I've been home. I want to start a family. I need to have people that I look after and who look after me, just like I did in the Army. Even though fatherhood terrifies me, because I want to be a better father than my father was for me, I long to have a house filled with children and love.

My hand reaches for my cock and I envision Tammy as my wife, pulling a pie out of the oven while our children wait at the kitchen table for dessert. I would go up behind her, pressing my body against her delicious curves, and kiss the back of her neck. She would giggle and give me a glance that promised an even sweeter dessert once the children were in bed.

An image of Tammy giving me a striptease, a wicked smile on her lips and swaying her full hips as she peels lacy lingerie off and throws them to the floor, fills me with such a desire that I gasp for breath as I grab my cock tighter, pumping it harder and harder as I imagine losing myself deep in Tammy's hot pussy. I imagine her bending over the bed, spreading her legs and exposing her most private parts to me.

I remember the curve of her ass as I saw it today, and a primal heat takes over my body and I grip the wall of the shower to keep from falling over. The water in the shower starts to cool, but I can't stop what I've started. I stroke my hard cock faster and harder, not able to slow down and savor this fantasy of Tammy. I slide my hand over the head of my cock and then I'm groaning and coming all over the shower, my body quaking as if I just stepped on an IED.

I step out of the shower, having made the biggest decision of my life. Tammy will be mine and nothing will stand in the way between us. Not even her brother.

TAMMY

Today has officially been the longest day of my life. Work has kept me busy, but my mind keeps drifting back to Johnny. It hurts my pride to have my brother insisting that I need an escort, but the fact of the matter is I can't wait to see Johnny again, even if he is a babysitter that my brother has sent.

Luke always warned me about Johnny. He was dangerous when I was in high school and he had a terrible reputation. Everyone assumed he would end up in prison before his twenty-first birthday.

"We just loved the arrangement you did for us last time! I told Stanley that we had to come back." My attention snaps back to my customer and I watch her sign the payment slip, then bundle the bouquet of flowers in her arms.

"Thank you so much, Louise. I really appreciate that." The smile on my face feels permanent. Adding joy to people's lives means so much to me. I love all the different flowers and working with beautiful things, but the real pleasure for me is creating things that other people love.

"Oh, and expect a call from my cousin Suzanne. She works for a property management company and she was saying how they need a new supplier for flowers. Of course I recommended you!"

"That is awesome! Thank you!"

I want to punch the air with joy! Landing a contract with a property management company, especially if it's one of the ones that manages corporate buildings downtown, would be an amazing client to have. That is a lot of weekly, repeat business. I'd be able to hire an assistant or two and build my business up faster.

Luke doesn't understand why I opened my shop here, in our old neighborhood, because it's not a fancy neighborhood at all. But the rent was cheap and this is a good way for me to get my business off the ground. It's also meaningful to me to have a business in the neighborhood I grew up in. Sense of community is important to me.

My back is to the door when the bell rings again, but my smile freezes and falls off my face when I see who it is. I've seen these boys roaming the neighborhood, clearly up to no good.

"Yo, fatty. We been watching you. Looks like you're having a good day. Also looks like you need someone to watch out for your business. Get what I'm saying?" He grins at me and it makes my skin crawl. I know exactly what he wants, but there's no way in hell I'm going to pay him supposed protection money. First, I'm not making much money. Second, I refuse to give in to bullying. Yet at the same time, I know they won't hesitate to damage my store if they don't get what they want.

I stifle a shiver as I listen to him. These are exactly the kind of guys that Luke wants to protect me from. With the way these guys are looking around my store and looking at me like I'm prey, I reluctantly admit that maybe Luke was right in sending Johnny to look out for me. Only thing, Johnny isn't here right now.

Maybe opening the store up here wasn't a great idea. I push down the feelings of fear and self-doubt, hoping beyond hope that I'm guarding my feelings in front of these thugs.

"Thanks," I say, doing my best to put on a brave face and smile politely at the thug and his friend, "but I'll pass. I'm barely scraping by, so you know."

As soon as the words are out of my mouth, I hate myself a little bit for trying to justify myself to this kid, and also for admitting that I'm not making a lot of money. The truth is I need a contract, like the one with the property management company, if I'm going to stay in business for more than the next six months. Fresh flowers don't come cheap and they don't have a long shelf life. All of my savings is in this little store and I don't have anything else to fall back on.

The bully clicks his tongue at me, practically laughing as he watches me and shakes his head. He rolls his weight from foot to foot, deliberately flexing his muscles as he does so. I have no doubts that he has the strength and willingness to destroy my store.

"You just think about it, fatty. We got our eye on you and we're never far away."

When I was little, Luke taught me how to fight. Yet the way this guy holds himself, I know that I'm no match for him, not to mention that he probably fights dirty. This is precisely the kind of guy Luke was warning me about yesterday.

Ignoring, again, the slur about my weight, I will myself to meet his gaze and stare at him. Him and his friend don't move for a long second, but then he barks a laugh and turns and walks out the door.

As soon as they're out of sight, I exhale and put both of my hands on the edge of the counter, steadying myself. Adrenaline surges through me, amplifying my fear. I don't have roll-down gates for the windows of my shop and I can't afford them.

Fuck! What am I going to do?

THE NEXT TIME the doorbell jingles, I'm again standing with my back to the door. My body freezes and I drop a plastic bucket of flowers, causing water and flowers to slop across my floor.

"Dammit," I mutter, carefully turning toward the front of the store. It's not going to do any good if I slip and hurt myself.

"Can I help… Oh, Johnny, hi. I just need to clean this up."

"Hello, Tammy. Are you okay? You look stressed."

"I'm fine," I lie. I know it's stubbornness, but I don't want to admit to Johnny that I need help.

I bend to pick up the flowers and put them back in to the bucket. Thankfully, none of the petals are bruised, so I can still use them.

"Tammy. You are not okay." Johnny's voice is low and he takes a step toward me, careful not to step on any flowers. I look at his stature and muscles, and have a flash of a thought that I hire him to work here, though of course this is not the kind of job for him. Still, I'd feel safer and, more enticingly, I'd get to spend more time with him.

"Look. If you want to help me mop, you can help me mop." I bristle with surprise at the raw concern I hear in his voice, then walk towards the storage closet, but Johnny meets me at the closet and puts his hand on the door, preventing me from opening it.

"You are too upset for just having dropped some flowers. When you heard the bell of the door, you were scared. I know you well enough to know that you are not a scared person. What happened?"

I look at the wall of muscle that is Johnny and realize that nothing else is happening today, unless I talk to him. His brown eyes blaze with a fierceness that makes me pause. It's like he wants to solve my problem and that he's mad because I'm scared.

I look down at the ground and take a deep breath. I hate that it makes me feel weak to admit that I need help. Luke always looked out for me in high school, until he enlisted. He always made me feel safe, but he always made me feel like I needed someone to look after me. Luke meant well, but I've always wanted to prove to him and myself that I could take care of myself, that I didn't need someone looking after me.

"Some... A couple of guys came into the store today. I've seen them around the neighborhood and I know they're just bullies. They're demanding protection money and I can't pay it. I don't even want to pay it, but right now I don't think there are any other options. I've sunk everything into this store, and I can't just close it and open up somewhere else."

The words flow out of my mouth as I describe what happened earlier. I didn't think it would be this easy to talk about this, especially with Johnny, but I feel safe with him. I'm blindsided by the realization that I can trust him...that I want to trust him.

When I finally stop talking, I notice that Johnny is opening and closing his fists, and that his breathing is rapid and uneven.

"I'll figure it out," I say, turning toward the storage closet so that I can grab the mop. Johnny steps away from the door and I get to mopping. But there's something unsettling about Johnny not saying anything. I can feel tension rolling off of him.

"I'm fairly sure I know who you mean. I ran into some boys last night who fit the profile." He says while I finish mopping the floor.

I grab my bag, and then mentally cross my fingers that I don't come in tomorrow and find my store destroyed. "I'm ready to head out."

Johnny looks up and down the streets as I lock my store and take a moment to look in at my store. *This. This is mine.* I feel incredibly protective of my store, but I don't know how I can protect it against the thugs.

"Everything is clear right now." Johnny momentarily puts his hand at the bottom of my back as we move into the sidewalk and walk toward my apartment. I gasp a little and bite my lip when I feel a jolt of desire electrify my body.

We walk in silence down the deserted street. My body relaxes as we walk together. It feels natural to walk with him, like it's something we've done a thousand times before.

"What did you do in the Army? Or can you talk about it? I know that Luke can't talk about what he does."

Johnny step falters for a moment and I instinctively reach out and grab his arm.

"We…we shouldn't talk about that. That's not something you want to hear," he says, lightly touching my bare fingers with his hand. The look in his eyes softens, but then a wall comes down over his eyes.

"I want to know, Johnny. Really. I know war and what you guys do isn't pretty."

Johnny takes a long look at me, then turns his head and scans the street again.

"I'm a sharpshooter," he finally says, his pace not faltering.

"But what do you... Oh." It all clicks rapidly in my head. These days, there is only one thing you shoot at in war. I let it roll through my mind, the fact that his job was to kill people.

It's surprising to discover that I'm not scared. If anything, I'm fascinated.

"Are you okay?" Johnny quickly turns his head at me and his eyes flash in the street lights.

"Yeah. I'm okay. That's unexpected."

"Turns out shooting was something I'm very good at. And I have the temperament for the job."

"But you don't seem...cold. I've always assumed that sharpshooters were shut off emotionally. You're not like that. At least, I don't think you are."

"Let's sit." Johnny sighs, slowing his walking pace. He lightly touches my arm and nods toward a stoop. I sit on the cold stone stair and pull my scarf tighter around my throat.

"You can tell me. It's okay."

"It's… When I'm on assignment, I shut down my emotions. There's no way to do the job otherwise. But… The job started exacting a price on me. Most guys in the job, they end up in private security or freelancers. What I was doing was bringing out a side of me that scared me. So, I finished my tour and came home."

I sit in silence as I listen to Johnny. I try to imagine what it must be like, but all I can envision are scenes from movies I've seen – crouching on the ground, hiding behind bushes on the top of a hill, waiting.

"Are you okay?"

Johnny makes a choked sound, but nods his head. His eyes are looking away from me, but his body tenses and shows the struggle that he's feeling. An urge to protect him, to give him comfort, rises up in me. I can't protect him in the physical way he can protect me, but the urge to protect him emotionally and help him move past what he's done is suddenly the most important thing in the world to me.

"Getting there. Maybe."

"Do you know what you're going to do, now that you're home?"

"Not particularly. Working private security isn't what I want to do, but there aren't many good options out there. It's not like I have a college education or another skill to fall back on."

"If there's anything I can do for you, just let me know," I say, reaching out and putting my hand on his leg.

"I appreciate that, Tammy. I really do."

I look at Johnny and feel like a fool. What could I do for him? He's the one sent to protect *me*.

We talk for a few more minutes, before it gets too cold to keep sitting on the cold stone. The more time I spend with him, the more I feel something between us. I can barely put words to it, but it's that sensation of having found something – someone – and that the stars and moon are aligned just right, and something magic is in the air. It's more than just finding him attractive. *Could there really be potential between Johnny and me?*

"Penny for your thoughts?"

I look at Johnny and realize that we're in front of my apartment building. A street light shines behind him, emphasizing how tall and imposing he is. He stands facing me, his jacket falling open, and all I want to do is snuggle inside his coat and against his body, feeling his body heat and smelling the scent of his skin. I clench my thighs together as my body flames with desire for him.

"Oh, just thinking about everything." I'm utterly unable to tell him that I was just wondering what he looks like naked. I smile at him and lightly place my hand on his arm. "Thanks for walking me home. I'll see you tomorrow."

"Absolutely. I'm available whenever you need me." Johnny pauses for a moment, the adds, "You can contact me anytime. Anytime."

JOHNNY

Fuck. Coming home wasn't supposed to be like this.

All I wanted to do was lay low and figure out the next part of my life. An inheritance from my grandma has me set up so long as I don't blow it all fast. It's enough for a modest lifestyle. While a fancy lifestyle isn't my thing, I do want to be able to enjoy nice things.

And being around Tammy makes me want to give her nice things and make her life better.

Fuck. Tammy.

I want to curse and thank Luke for throwing us together. A relationship with anyone hasn't been on my agenda at all, but Tammy… She makes me want to build a family. It's goddamn terrifying to consider sharing myself and being open with another person, but she pushes through all the walls I have built like they are nothing. She's not even trying, it's just who she is. She's sweet and smart and gorgeous. I want nothing more than to get lost in her curves and be part of her life – every day, every year. Forever.

I'm going to build a family with her. There's just one thing I need to do, first.

"Luke, buddy. How's things?"

I press my hand on my knee to steady the nervous bouncing. There's no way in hell he's going to be happy about what I have to tell him. He gave more than one boy a black eye and the promise of more, just for looking at Tammy in high school.

"About the same. You know how it is." His voice muffles on the phone and I can hear soldiers in the background yelling at each other. There's always a lot of yelling, when you're out in the desert. Part of me misses deployment, but I also know coming home was the right decision. I was losing myself in a way that I saw lead other men into ruin, and I knew that I wanted and needed more. "How's Tammy? You helping her out?"

I take a deep breath and pray for the best.

"Yeah, Tammy's good. She's doing good, that flower shop of hers."

"It's crazy she's back in the neighborhood. But she's stubborn as a mule."

I laugh at that. "That's for sure. She told me off for walking her home. You might want to avoid talking to her for a bit."

"Well, it's for her own good."

"It was the right thing to do, Luke. I don't mind helping. You know I'd do anything for you. For her, too."

"Wait. Are there problems?" Luke's voice tenses and focuses like a laser. The hairs on my arm stand up when he's like this. His focus is what makes him an excellent and effective soldier.

"Some local thugs are demanding protection money. Don't worry. I'll take care of them."

"Motherfucker!" Luke's voice explodes and I have to pull the phone from my ear. "You do whatever it takes, Johnny. Whatever it fucking takes. No one messes with my sister!"

"Don't worry, Luke. I've got her covered."

"Keep me posted. Look," he says, his voice muffling again as he yells at someone, "I need to go. Keep me apprised of the situation."

"Sure thing. But hold on Luke. There's something you should know."

"What?" His voice is distracted. This can go really well or to fucking hell, but I gotta tell him. I can't keep secrets from my best friend. "Make it quick. I gotta hustle."

"Let me finish before you say anything, okay?" I pace around my small apartment, knocking my shin on the coffee table. Luke doesn't say anything, so I start talking fast. "I like your sister. And I mean that the way I like her is more than she's just your sister. There's something special about her and I've liked her for a long time. I'm going to make her mine."

"Johnny." The warning tone in his voice makes my skin crawl. I'm glad he's on the other side of the world right now. "You hurt her and you know I will kill you. They won't find your body."

"Luke, if anyone is going to get hurt, it's me. I'm not asking for your permission, because it's not respectful to her. I can't ignore what I feel for her. If she will have me, I will make her the happiest woman and mother on the planet. I will worship her with every breath that I have left in this body."

"What does Tammy have to say about all of this?"

I take a deep breath. "I haven't actually asked her anything and nothing has happened, yet. But man, there is something there. I can feel it. I wanted you to hear it from me, first, Luke. I know you're protective of her and that you love her deeply. Luke," I hesitate, scared to put my emotions into words. But it's the only way for Luke to know how serious I am. "I love her. I don't understand it because it's happened so fast. But she's the one. She is the only one."

Luke is silent for a long moment, his breath steady on the phone. I sit down and rub my shin, wincing when I touch the bruise forming from cracking it on the coffee table.

"I appreciate you telling me. Keep my sister happy and do right by her."

"I will, Luke. I swear to you."

We end the call and I exhale deeply, releasing all of the tension that built up before talking to Luke. There's no way that I'm not going to pursue his sister, but I knew I couldn't hide this from him.

Now, I just have to convince Tammy. And she scares me more than her brother. I'd take a beating from her brother if I had to, but if she says 'no,' then my life is lost.

LANA LOVE

IT'S BECOME that late afternoon is my favorite part of the day, because that's when I get to see Tammy.

I take my time walking to the flower store, enjoying the crisp fall air and just being in the neighborhood again. It's always a shock to the system, coming home from a deployment. It's hard to break the habits of always being on and looking over your shoulder. Home, I don't have my brothers looking out for me.

As I turn onto the street were Tammy's flower store is, I see three guys leaving her shop. I recognize their distinctive way of walking, the one that looks like a mix between jerky movements and a rolling body, before I even see their faces. My body instinctively tenses at the sight of them. They are the ones that were harassing my Tammy and the ones who mouthed off to me the other night.

I force myself to count to ten when I feel how tightly my fingers are balled into fists. This kind of reaction is what got me into trouble before the Army. But the boys walk in the other direction and I let them go. Finding out how Tammy is doing is more important right now. She didn't fully admit it yesterday, but I could see how shook up she was after their first visit.

The bell above the door jingles as I walk in and I see her wrapping up a beautiful bouquet of flowers and smiling stiffly as she gives a woman a receipt.

"Have a good day! I'll see you next week."

The customer turns and walks out to her car on the street. Tammy looks at me and a different smile creases her lips, the kind of smile that you have when you see someone that is special to you.

"Hey, Johnny. You're early." She walks around to the front of the store, wiping her hands on her apron. The hair on the back of my neck stands on end when I see how badly her hands are shaking.

"You're trembling. Are you okay? I saw those three guys leaving the store. I recognize them. Are they the ones that have been bothering you?" It's a struggle to control my base urge to go and pound those guys into the pavement, until even their mothers couldn't recognize them.

Tammy looks away and shakes her hands nervously. It pierces my heart to see her so clearly scared.

"Tammy, sweetheart. It's okay, come here." I open my arms and she immediately rushes into them, her body trembling. I wrap my arms around her, the urge to protect her overwhelming every part of my being. Her arms wrap around my waist and she presses her curvy body against mine, and a whole different set of feelings and reactions awaken in me.

"I... I'm sorry. I don't know what came over me. I don't know why those guys bother me as much as they do. I know they're just petty bullies, but I can't help being scared that they're going to bust up my store."

"It's okay," I say quietly, reaching up and stroking her hair, and leaning down to kiss the top of her head.

Tammy leans into me and tilts her face up to mine, her hand wrapping around my neck and pulling my face down to hers. Her full lips press against mine and it's like being able to breathe for the very first time. I pull her closer to me, returning her kiss with the fierceness that surprises even me. I press my tongue to her lips, and she parts them and greets me with her sweet tongue.

I can't hold back the raw desire that her kiss unleashes, and my hands slide down her back and cup her luscious ass. As I feel Tammy press against me, her mouth and her body hungry for more, my cock stiffens and demands more. Our kiss deepens and when we break apart, we're gasping for breath as we look into each other's eyes.

"That was… That was amazing."

"That was something that we need to finish somewhere more private." I shift my weight, my erection pressing painfully against my jeans. "Are you finished for the day?" I can feel an almost desperation in my question, because I need to be with Tammy with nothing between us. No clothes, just the two of us exploring each other's bodies and making love until we can't walk anymore.

Color rises high in Tammy's cheeks and the happiness in her eyes makes her even more beautiful.

"I can close up early. I don't have any other orders to be picked up and anything else can definitely wait until tomorrow." The smile on her lips is wicked and I know even more, that she is absolutely the right woman for me. I can't wait to find out how she likes to touch, how she tastes, how she screams out when she comes.

I chuckle as I watch her speed through her closing routine, making sure all the flowers have enough water, locking the till up in a safe in the back office.

"Okay. I'm ready if you are." She pulls on her coat and wraps her scarf around her neck. I can't fucking wait to peel her clothes off and see her glorious body. There's a little gap between her scarf and the top of her blouse, and just that glimpse of the top of her chest brings out the caveman in me. My cock strains even more as my mind imagines unbuttoning her blouse, and seeing and touching her bare skin. She has the perfect body for being a mother, and I can't wait to fill up her belly with babies.

"I've been ready for you for a long time."

Tammy blushes a deep crimson as we leave the flower store, and she locks the door securely. I wrap my arm around her shoulder and pull her close to me. She fits perfectly under my arm and my heart beats faster when she threads her arm under my jacket and around my waist. It's as perfect a moment as a moment can be. The air between us is electric with the promise and the future, and there's nothing more in this world that I can ask for.

"So, Tammy. Tell me about your dreams for the flower store. What's your goal? I want to know everything about it."

She looks up at me and her blue eyes flash with excitement and pride.

"Well, I have a lead on a contract for doing some corporate work. I'd love to land a couple of contracts like that, because then I can expand my business, and then—"

"And then you'll be able to pay up, like a good little fatty. Maybe you'll buy less food and then get pretty." The voice that taunts us is behind us. Tammy's body stiffens under my arm, and she inhales a deep breath and holds it. Fear is rolling off her and I swear on everything that I'm going to create a world for her where she doesn't have to be afraid of anything.

I turn on my heel and face three young men. They barely look old enough to be out of high school. The leader of the three looks at me, a smug smile on his mouth. He's a worse version of me at his age. Listening to the way he talks to and about Tammy makes me see red and pushes all my buttons for how much I hate bullies.

And I know how to deal with bullies.

"About that." I take a step toward him, and swing my fist at his face.

TAMMY

"Oh my God!"

I watch as Johnny punches the thug who was just a second ago looking at me like he owned me. As much as I hate violence, it's more than a little satisfying to watch as he stumbles and grabs at his face.

"Yo what the fuck?" He yells as blood pours from his nose. "Do you even know who I am? You sure that fatty is worth what you've got coming to you, now?"

Johnny takes a step closer to the kid and the tone of his voice is something that I've never heard before. His voice is low and the steadiness with which he speaks frightens me.

"Kid, that's cute. You don't know who *you* are dealing with. I'm back from three tours in the Middle East. You are nothing compared to the insurgents I've eliminated. If you come anywhere near Tammy again, or if I hear you say anything nasty about this beautiful woman, I will come for you. And what's just happened here, right now? That's nothing compared to what I will do to you. Do I make myself clear?"

"Johnny! Watch out!" I scream when I see one of the boys lunge at Johnny, a knife glinting in his hand.

Johnny moves his body rapidly, thrusting out one of his strong arms and expertly knocking the knife to the ground. He kicks the knife so that it ends up by my feet. I kick it toward the curb and hear it clatter down into the storm drain. When I look back at Johnny and the second kid, Johnny has his arm twisted behind his back in his voice is speaking in the boy's ear.

"Do I make myself clear?"

"Yes, sir." The boy's voice shakes and he cowers away from Johnny.

Johnny releases him and pushes him back towards the boy's friends.

"Are we clear about what's just happened here?"

"Yes, sir," the first boy says, looking down at the ground. "We won't bother her again. We're sorry, ma'am."

My mouth falls open in shock as I listen to the boy. I have no idea what to say, so I say nothing.

"Good. Now that we've got that out of the way, you're the boys who robbed Parker's, right?"

None of the boys answer immediately, but the way they shift their eyes away from Johnny tells the full story.

"That's what I thought. I'll give you two options. You stop this intimidation you've been doing in the neighborhood or we can deal with this between the four of us. We don't have to get the cops involved, but I can guarantee you that going up against me is a fight you can't win." The steely look in Johnny's eyes and the controlled anger in his voice command the boys' attention. "Are we clear on this? Do you understand what will happen if I hear that any of you are bothering anyone else in this neighborhood?"

The boys are slow to speak, but they look at each other and then nod slowly.

"Yes, we do. We'll leave the neighborhood alone."

"Good. Now get out of here. I don't want to see you again."

I watch as the boys turn and leave in a hurry, then Johnny comes over to me and puts his arm around my shoulders again, and it's a very possessive gesture. His height and strong body make me feel like nothing bad can touch me. And I like it more than I ever thought possible.

Tears of happiness and gratitude well up in my eyes. It's impossible to contain the emotions that I feel right now. I feel loved and protected, and like I belong.

"Sweetheart, why are you crying?" Johnny wraps his arms around me and hugs me so tightly that I can barely breathe. I sob into his chest and he gently strokes my hair, whispering into my ear and calming me down.

"No one has ever done that for me. I didn't think anyone except my brother would ever care for me that much. You've saved my store for me."

"It's okay, Tammy. I will always protect you. I never want anything to hurt you. Now let's get home."

"Do you need to talk about what happened?"

Johnny is sitting next to me, holding me tightly.

"I… I'm not sure." I think for a moment. "Honestly. It was surprising to see how you dealt with those boys. It was a side of you that I've never seen before."

"Were you scared?"

"In a way, yes? I mean, it was intense to watch you fight. I don't like fighting, but… But I like how I felt protected. It meant so much to me that you stood up for me. I never thought anyone would feel so…so protective of me."

"Tammy. I will protect you forever. I will do everything in my power not to let something bad happen to you." He looks into my eyes and an intense moment passes between us. I know that he's not lying.

"I trust you, Johnny. And thank you. You make me feel so special." I reach out and caress his jaw, then lean in and kiss him on the lips.

Something deep inside of me opens up and I realize it's my heart. I love Johnny. A complex set of emotions overwhelms me. I've been interested in men before, but it's never been like this. I've never wanted to share everything about myself with someone, much less think about a long-term future. I've never felt comfortable with another man. But with Johnny, it just feels right and I know that he is the one.

"It's always been you, Johnny. I liked you when we were younger and I love you now."

Johnny's eyes widen and the look on his face changes. I see a vulnerability in his eyes and it goes straight to my heart.

"I love you, too, Tammy. With all of my heart. I will love you and protect you, forever. I want to build a family with you."

"Oh, Johnny! Me, too!"

He pulls my hand and moves my body so that I'm straddling his lap. I've never done this before, but it makes me feel powerful. I press my chest against his and run my fingers over his neck and down to his chest, letting my fingers slide inside the top of his shirt. I gasp as my fingers graze the hard muscles of his chest.

"You are so beautiful, Tammy. You are an incredible woman. I will treat you better than any man has ever treated you."

I hesitate for a moment and look away from Johnny. Do I tell him? How do I tell him?

"Sweetheart, what's wrong?"

"I… Well the thing is, I've never been with anybody else. I've never had a boyfriend."

"Tammy, what? Do you mean that you're a… That you're a virgin?"

I force myself to look in Johnny's eyes, despite feeling totally embarrassed. Of course, someone amazing like him wants a woman with experience. There's a look of surprise in his eyes as he looks at me and I feel like I've said the wrong thing.

"Yes," I say, pulling away from him. But when I try to move back to the couch and away from his lap, he wraps his arms around me even tighter and won't let go.

"Tammy. Why do you look so scared and ashamed? There is nothing wrong with this. Fuck. I'm honored that I will be your first, that I will be your only."

"Really?" My voice squeaks. I'm confused by the smile on his lips, and when he kisses me gently on the lips, a wave of relief rushes through me.

"Yes, really," he teases. "In fact, I love that you're a virgin. I love that you saved yourself because you wanted to make it special. I love that I will know you in a way that no other man ever will."

I move my hips against on his lap, trying to be bold about what I want. I shiver in delicious anticipation at how hard he is. *I make him feel that way. Me!*

"I never wanted to have sex just to have sex," I admit, tugging at Johnny's shirt. "I've always wanted my first time to be with somebody special and to be special. And you are the most special man I've ever met."

A sound like a growl comes out of Johnny and it stirs a need deep within me. I am going to give myself to him, utterly and completely. He is the only man for me.

"Make me yours," I whisper.

JOHNNY

The moment that Tammy told me that she was untouched, my whole world tilted in the best possible way. I feel even more fiercely protective about her. She is my chance to start a new life and I know I will never find a woman more perfect than she is.

"We need to go to bed," my voice is heavy as I look at Tammy and see the excitement and trust in her eyes. "I want to be able to see all of your glorious body."

Tammy smiles and stands up, extending her hand to me in invitation. Without a moment's hesitation I take her soft hand in mine and smile as she leads me toward her bedroom.

"Leave the lights on," I say when she reaches for the light switch. "I want to see all of you."

"But I'm not too…" She looks down at her body and hesitates.

"Tammy, you're perfect. I don't know what anybody else has told you about your figure, but you have absolutely nothing to be hesitant about. You're…fuck. You're the sexiest woman I've ever seen."

A shy smile plays on her lips and I see confidence building in her. My hands pull at her blouse, and Tammy giggles and bats my hands away.

"I don't know if you want to be all romantic and take your time, but I can't wait, Johnny. I need you now. Can we do the romantic lovemaking another time?"

I stand in front of her, more than a little bit stunned. "I want your first time to be special. I don't want to be fast and dirty, because you deserve more than that."

Tammy rapidly takes off her clothes before I can stop her. Her body is even more beautiful and sexy than I imagined. Her curves are soft and her creamy skin is the most beautiful thing I have ever seen. I'm transfixed by a sprinkling of freckles across her stomach.

"Johnny, this is still special and this is the way I want it." She reaches down and caresses my cock through my pants and I swear I nearly come just from that. "I want my first time to be fast and dirty."

I pull my clothes off as fast as I can, because she's not just my woman, she's the most perfect woman ever.

I pick her up and lay her on the bed, and climb over her curvy body. I'm dying to plunge my cock deep inside of her sweet pussy and lose myself in her. I can't wait for her belly to swell with our baby.

"Your wish is my command."

TAMMY

I never thought I'd feel comfortable being naked in front of a man, especially a man as fit and sexy as Johnny, but I am. He makes me feel so secure and sexy – I've discovered a part of me that I never knew *could* exist.

Johnny's body is a wall of chiseled muscle and tattoos, and seeing his body makes me understand what my girlfriends mean when they talk about lust. But this is more powerful than lust, because I love Johnny, too.

"I'll ask you about these tattoos another time," I say, smiling up at Johnny and spreading my legs for him. "But right now, I need this." I move my hand down and take his thick cock in my fingers, wrapping my fingers around his hard length and feeling his cock move.

"Tighter," he says, his voice jagged.

I squeeze his cock with my fingers as I stroke him, adjusting my movements to his reactions. When his cock twitches or he moans, I repeat what I've done. I'm eager to learn how to please him.

"I can't wait to learn what you like." I gasp as Johnny puts his hand between my legs, sliding his fingers through my hot wetness and teasing at my most intimate place. Pleasure lights up my nerve endings and I need more of Johnny. I need to be one with Johnny. "Oh, God. I need you inside of me!"

Johnny leans his head down and kisses me, then presses his hips toward mine. His cock bumps at my pussy and nothing has ever meant more to me than this moment. Stars explode behind my eyes as he pushes into me and I feel myself stretching around him. It hurts more than a little, but I wiggle my hips, hungry to have him deep inside of me and to release the tension that has been building inside of me since he walked back into my flower store.

"Don't be gentle." I look up into his dark eyes and push my hips up to meet his. His eyes crease and I see a conflict behind them, but he leans down and kisses me as he plunges deep inside of me.

Johnny thrusts quicker and quicker, his hips moving as if he was dancing. Every stroke sets off a new explosion of pleasure within me and it makes me scream. It feels so good and giving this special first-time to him seals my love and commitment for him.

"Oh!" I laugh and gasp as he wraps his arms around me and flips us so that I'm on top.

"I want to watch you over me and watch your body as you come." Johnny reaches up and roughly massage my breasts, running his thumb over my painfully erect nipples and making me squirm with even more need. Seeing his raw desire unleashes something deeper in me and more pleasure rises up inside of me.

"This is so new…and so…I don't even have words for how good this feels!"

"We are only just beginning," Johnny says, moving his hips and stoking the fire in me as our bodies move together.

I grab his hands and hold them tightly, arching myself into his body, desperately yearning to feel him deeper inside of me. My hips move faster and faster, in a primal way that shocks and delights me. I let myself go over to pleasure and sensation, doing what feels natural and hoping that this feels as amazing for Johnny as it does for me.

My breathing quickens and my body jerks as an overwhelming tension rapidly builds up inside of me. In this moment, there is nothing more than Johnny and my love for him, and the pleasure that is about to erupt in my body.

"I… something is happening in me." I don't even recognize the moans and cries of pleasure coming out of my mouth. "I feel like I'm about to explode."

Johnny's dark eyes blaze and his mouth stretches into a proud smile. He thrusts up into me, deeper and faster, so much that I'm seeing stars again. I hold his hands tightly, every nerve ending in my body lit up like the Fourth of July.

"Let yourself explode, baby. Let me see you come for the very first time."

My hips buck and jerk as I ride Johnny's thick cock and feel him rubbing something inside of me that makes me want to never stop doing this. Releasing my hands, Johnny grabs my ass and pulls me a little lower to him, then latches his mouth on one of my breasts and sucks so hard and licks at my aching nipple that I scream and scream.

I look down at Johnny as my body explodes over him and waves of pleasure vibrate through my body. His face is red, and then he's thrusting up into me, deeper than before, and I nearly black out from how good he feels. My hips rock back and forth over his cock and his body shakes and he moans loudly as he slams his cock into me and comes.

The look of tenderness in Johnny's eyes goes straight to my core and I know that this night has created a special bond between us. We will be together, forever, and there's not a force in this world that can separate us.

"I… That was the best thing ever." I collapse on top of him and we roll over, holding each other fiercely as our breathing returns to normal.

"Sweetheart, that was just the beginning." Johnny runs his hands over my body and I giggle from how sensitive and ticklish my skin feels.

"That's good," I say, leaning toward him and kissing him slowly. "I feel like I need some more practice. And," I grab his hand and place it on my stomach, "I want a baby in here. Let's build an enormous family."

Johnny smiles and hugs me tightly.

"Being a family man is what I've always wanted. It's taken me a long time to get my shit together, but I'm here now, with you, and I'll never want for anything more. I will give you anything and everything you ask for."

The intensity of this moment brings tears to my eyes, and Johnny kisses each of them away.

"Then let's work on that baby. And this time, Johnny, let's take it slow."

Johnny reaches between my legs and slowly stroking me with his strong fingers. Everything is swollen and sensitive, but I need more. So much more. A deep flame builds inside of me and I already know that this is going to be more intense and powerful than what we just finished. It's scary, but I'm ready.

"Your wish is my command, sweetheart. I love you with my entire body and soul."

EPILOGUE

*D*amn! When did you become such a great cook?"

Johnny laughs and Luke closes his eyes and leans back in his chair, his hand rubbing his belly. Johnny grabs Luke's empty beer bottle and heads toward the kitchen.

"I've learned a few things," I say, looking to Johnny and smiling as he grabs fresh beers for him and Luke from the fridge. "Hey babe? Grab me some more sparkling cider while you're in there?"

"Johnny, man. I came home, ready to brawl with you for going after my sister," he shakes his head, a laugh escaping from him, "but you two? My God you're great together."

"You know, I had a say in all of this, too, dear brother." I roll my eyes. Truth is, I like that he's protective of me.

Luke has always been there for me, but he's never been overbearing about it. Well, except for maybe in high school, when he chased all the boys – including Johnny – away from me.

"She was worth the wait." Johnny cracks opens the beers and hands one to Luke, then puts his down and stands behind my chair, then puts down my drink next to me. I instantly relax when he puts his hands on my shoulders and lightly massages my tense muscles.

"Stop it, both of you," I laugh, putting my hand on Johnny's and looking up at him. Even now a year after he walked back into my life, it still takes my breath away that we found each other and are so deeply in love. "You talk like I'm the prize of the world."

"You *are* the prize of the world. And I'm the luckiest man in existence." Johnny leans down and kisses my neck, then rubs my very pregnant belly.

"Remind me of that the next time I ask you to cook dinner," I tease, running my hand along his neck.

"As much as I hate to admit it," Luke says, "you two are great together. Just remember, Johnny, you hurt my sister..."

"Yeah, yeah. And you'll hurt me." Johnny rolls his eyes. I know how often Luke has told him this, because he's told me this, too. "But Luke, you say that like you could take me."

I rub my baby belly and shake my head as Johnny and Luke get into a heated argument about who would win, in a variety of terrain. Forest. Desert. Antarctica. City. Ocean.

"Oh! The baby moved! Luke, do you want to feel it kick?"

Luke's eyes focus on me like a laser, then drop to my stomach. He pushes his chair back and walks around our dining table, then looks down at my stomach with a look bordering on disbelief.

"You can touch my stomach, you know," I tease, grabbing his hand and putting it on my belly. "There! The baby just kicked. Did you feel it?"

"You're going to be an uncle soon, man." Johnny slaps Luke's shoulder and Luke looks like he doesn't know what to say or to do. He's been home for a month now, but it seems like he has a hard time imagining his little sister married and about to have a baby.

"One day, you're going to have a wife of your own and babies on the way."

Johnny and I laugh as Luke shudders and goes back to his chair, picking up his beer and taking a long drink.

"I don't know about that, man."

"Just you wait, Luke. Once you find the right woman, you'll know and everything you know about your life will turn upside down. Reconnecting with your sister reminded me just how much I wanted a family of my own. It also reminded me of how perfect she is and how beautiful. Life just makes sense with her and I can't imagine life any other way."

No matter how many times Johnny tells me how beautiful I am and how much he loves my body, I still blush like crazy. He is such the perfect man for me, and I still thank my lucky stars that Luke made him come and look out for me.

"You can stop right there, Johnny," Luke says, putting his hand up in the morning. "You're about to go into territory that is dangerous. I don't need to hear you talk about my sister like that."

Johnny and I laugh, and he reaches across the table and squeezes my hand. I look in his eyes and I can't wait until we are alone in bed. Some of my girlfriends say that they lost their sex drive when they got pregnant, but it is so not like that for me. Even eight months pregnant, I need the intimate connection with Johnny, not to mention he loves my baby belly. He thinks it's the hottest thing when I'm on top.

"Johnny, help me clear the table? Then I'll let you two catch up some more. I need to rest anyway and I also need to put the finishing touches on a bid for a new client."

LANA LOVE

"You can take a night off, you know?" Luke smiles as he picks up plates and silverware and follows me into the kitchen.

We move around the kitchen in our practiced rhythm and I feel even luckier to have a man who helps me with things like loading the dishwasher and clearing the dinner table. He rinses his hands after we finish and I stand next to him and wrap my arms around his arm.

"I miss being able to hug you properly." I lean into Johnny and he wraps his arm around my shoulder and pulls me close to him. "Don't stay up too late. I'll keep the bed warm for you."

Johnny takes my jaw in his hands and tilts my head up to his, and then kisses me slowly.

"Have I told you lately how much I love you? How I'm the luckiest man in the world?"

"Maybe you have, but I never get tired of hearing it. Have I told you how much I love you and how I thank my lucky stars every day that we found each other again?"

Johnny smiles, then kisses me again. I kiss hungrily, licking and sucking at his tongue, enjoying the taste of beer. Kissing Johnny after he's been drinking, it's as close as I get to alcohol these days.

"You have, but I never get tired of it, either."

EPILOGUE

"You behave for uncle Luke now, you hear?" Johnny hands me the overnight bag for the kids and I open it and triple check that everything is there.

"Everything is going to be fine, sister. Abigail and I are ready for anything. And if we need anything, we'll just go out and get it. It's no big deal."

"I just can't help being nervous, you know? It's going to be the first night that we've been away from the kids."

Abigail smiles warmly at me and walks over to Luke and puts her arm around his waist. When Luke looks at her, I see something shift in his eyes and it's as clear as day how deeply in love he is with Abigail. It warms my heart to see him so happy and I know that Abigail will make him a wonderful wife and a fantastic mother to their children.

"Tammy, you deserve this night off. We all know how much you and Johnny do for the kids and it's overdue for you two to have a date night."

I smile and nod my head, knowing that she's right. I zip up the bag and hand it over to her.

"Okay, okay. I get the message," I smile and then look down to Peter and Paul. My heart always swells in indescribable ways when I look at our children. They're such beautiful boys and the absolute center of our universe.

"Are you all still here?" Johnny says, joining us in the entryway of the house and wiping sawdust off of his hands. "You two are like family, but we're looking forward to a night for just the two of us."

Johnny and I squat down to Peter and Paul, to give them kisses and hugs. They look just like Johnny, with their dark eyes and almost-black hair. They're tall for their age and I'm already preparing myself for how quickly they are going to grow up. Abigail jokes that they'll be taller than I am by the time they're teenagers. She's probably right.

"Love you two." My voice chokes as I release them and we watch Luke and Abigail usher our children out to their car.

Johnny closes the front door quietly, then exhales. He comes over and wraps me in his arms, and comfort and love settle over me.

"It is strange, the twins not being here," Johnny whispers into my hair. "Though I can't tell you how much I've been looking forward to having time alone with you."

"Me, too, Johnny. I just want to lie in your arms and sleep late."

"Is that all you want to do?" Johnny laughs, pushing his hips against me.

I look up into his eyes and kiss his lips slowly.

"You know full well that's not all I want to do," I tease. I slide my hands down his back and cup his ass, pressing him even closer to me. "I want to lie in your arms after making slow love to you. If we do nothing but stay in bed, making love and just being together, that is absolutely fine with me."

"But what about the new crib? I know you want that done."

"The crib can wait. We've got a few more months before the boys have their sister."

"Well, your wish is my command, my gorgeous wife."

I giggle as he leads me up the stairs to our bedroom. Despite wanting to take our time, the moment we see our bed, we quickly strip off our clothes and we're making love fast and hard. Johnny holds me from behind as we lay on our sides, his cock pumping into me over and over again, hitting my g-spot perfectly with each thrust of his thick cock.

"Oh God!" I cry out, barely able to control my body as it thrashes against his, my orgasm overtaking me rapidly.

"Oh, Tammy!" Johnny cries out, his body twitching behind me as he fills me up with his come.

We carefully move around in the bed, once we catch our breath, so that I'm on my back and he's cuddling me from the side.

"You know," I say, placing my hand on Johnny's as he runs his hand over my belly, the look in his eyes deeply loving and protective. "That was just like the first time."

"You do this thing to me, woman, even after all these years. I can't contain myself with you."

"And just like that first time," I pull Johnny's head to mine and give him a slow, deep kiss, "we have all night ahead of us. So let's take this next one slow."

"Anything you want, my love, anything you want."

CLAIMING HER CURVES

LEAH

"Sure, Jake. I'll be over as soon as I finish up at work." I whisper into the phone, hoping my boss Mr. Whipple doesn't hear me. It's not like I can't talk and type at the same time, but he uses any excuse to get close to me and make me uncomfortable.

"Can't you leave early? There's a lot to do."

I glance toward Mr. Whipple's office, but cut my eyes away before he sees me. There isn't a question that I could finish my work early, but asking for a favor is asking for trouble. Even if I left now, it's not like these contracts and rental agreements couldn't wait until tomorrow morning.

"I wish. More than anything, I wish I could. I'll come over immediately after I get off, okay?"

We end our call and I go back to my work, focusing on it even more than usual. While it's okay if some of the work carries over until tomorrow, Mr. Whipple has less fuel for getting on my case if I can finish everything by the end of the day.

"Did I just hear you making a *personal* phone call, on the *company* phone, Leah?"

The sound of Mr. Whipple's voice makes the hair on my neck prickle and my blood pressure rise. I compose my face carefully before turning around to face him.

"I apologize. It was just a quick call from my cousin. You remember that my parents died recently," I add, blatantly and shamelessly playing the victim card. "He's helping me clear my parent's house and he was asking if I could leave work early. I said I had a lot of work and couldn't."

Mr. Whipple's eyes narrow at me. I know he knows about my parents, because this town isn't that small and he's not quite *that* narcissistic. I also know that despite not saying anything, he's more than a little resentful that I'm using a different real estate agent to sell my parent's house.

"Well," he says, his voice changing to a chilling drawl, "if you'd like to leave early, you could come in on the weekend and help me on a special project."

"No!" I blurt out, then instantly regret it. "I mean, thanks, but no. It's going to take us a while to go through everything and Jake would kill me if I didn't help all weekend. He's taken a week off work to come help me. Besides, I want to make sure all these contracts are finished today. I know this property deal is important and I want you to be prepared for your meeting."

His face is a mask and it bothers me when I can't read his emotions. More than once, he won't say anything about a situation, only to use it as fuel for manipulating me at a later date. He's a terrible boss, but there aren't that many jobs in town that don't involve working at the paper mill or the grocery store out by the interstate. I know I want to do more with my life than work here forever, but this will look better on my resume and I won't get sawdust in my lungs.

"Of course. I appreciate your diligence and commitment to the firm."

I plaster a smile on my face, then turn back to my computer and lose myself in ensuring all the details are entered correctly.

One day, I'll be married with kids and I won't have to deal with a creepy boss ever again. But until then, I have to figure a way out of this office and into a better life.

I just have to survive working for Mr. Whipple, first.

"I come bearing beer!" I call out as I carefully walk between the boxes quickly rising up in the entryway.

My parent's house isn't big, but it was modest enough and my mom kept it nicely decorated and orderly. It's about the smallest three-bedroom house you've ever seen. I'd love to move into this house, but I need the money from the sale to pay off their medical bills and funeral expenses. No one ever tells you how expensive getting old will be.

"Well aren't you a sight for sore eyes?"

"Ben? When did you get back?" My eyes blink rapidly as he takes the six-pack of beer out of my hands. He's several years older than I am, but I saw him occasionally when he was hanging out with my cousin Jake, who lived with my parents and me for a few years when he was in high school.

The moments I got to see Ben were the moments I lived for. He was my first crush and, if I'm honest, I've never quite gotten over him.

"Jake asked me to come over and help. I'm just living about an hour away and could use the change of scenery."

I smile and nod my head, my eyes zooming in on his finger and how he's not wearing a ring anymore. Ben laughs when he sees me looking at his hand.

"Yeah, Marlene and I broke up." His laugh dies quickly and a pained look shadows his eyes. I feel terrible that I'm happy his marriage ended.

"I'm sorry it didn't work out."

"It…" Ben walks over to the dining table and puts the beer on it. He opens a bottle and drains it in one long drink, then wipes the back of his hand across his mouth as he reaches for a fresh bottle. "It was a mistake. But, that's in the past. What about you? Your ring finger looks bare."

"Me?" I stammer and blush, totally flustered. What do you do when your first crush starts asking about your personal life? "No one special for me. One day, I suppose."

"You suppose?" Ben's eyes go wide, like I've just told him I've taken up particle physics as a hobby. "You're gorgeous and sweet and smart. How have you not been snapped up yet?"

Because I'm fat? I bite my tongue to keep from saying that aloud. The guys in town always go after the skinny girls and I've always felt like the girl that only gets attention when all the pretty girls are taken. Being single in a small town is a problem, but it's not a problem I've figured out how to solve.

"Uh, I guess I just haven't met the right guy."

"Jesus fucking Christ. Listen to you." Ben shakes his head. "I never imagined you were still single."

"What?" Ben thinks about me? I can barely wrap my mind around that.

"Hey hey. Look who finally showed up! Y'all can help me bring up boxes from the basement."

"Hey man," Ben says to Jake, before going over and handing him a beer. "How is it you're the one doing all the work?"

"Man, you remember that Leah's family took me in. They were more family to me than my own. She's like my sister – you know that."

Ben takes a long look at me, a smile still on his lips. "Yeah, I remember."

BEN

"So, where do you need me to start?" I smile as I look at Leah. It's been a hard week, but being in the same room as her makes my life better. It's unimaginable to think that she's still single.

"It's good of you to help, Ben. I really appreciate it. Helping Jake in the basement would be great. I'm scared of all the spiders down there."

"You got it." I follow Jake back downstairs, though what I really want is to be around Leah.

When Jake first asked me for help, I said no. I hate helping people move. But then I couldn't say no when he said it was to help Leah.

Leah's parents took Jake in when things got bad with his parents and living at home was dangerous. Her parents didn't even think twice – just cleared out the extra bedroom and welcomed him into their home and family like he'd always lived there. After we were out of high school, Jake said that if it wasn't for Leah's parents, he probably would have ended up like his dad – drunk and jobless, and a menace.

Even though she was a few years younger than me, I always found her attractive and appealing. But as a hormone-driven horndog while I was in high school, I knew that I couldn't settle down with one girl and a girl like Leah was definitely not the kind of girl that you fuck and dump. So as much as I wanted her, I stayed away. Leah has always been the type of woman that you want to settle down and build a family with.

By the time I *was* ready to settle down, I was living in the next city over and I met Marlene. Fuck. Just the memory of Marlene makes my blood boil. Marrying her was the absolute worst mistake of my life. Seeing Leah makes me realize just how badly I fucked up. I can already tell that she's the same person that she was in high school – smart, caring, and she has a figure that I want to spend my life touching.

Jake and I make quick work of the basement, gathering all of the boxes and then taking them upstairs and out to the back porch.

"So, what's the story with Leah? I thought she would've left this town and be married with kids by now."

Jake wipes his brow as he looks at me, and then laughs.

"You still carrying a torch for her? I remember you crushing on her in high school."

"Seeing her definitely brings back memories." I stack boxes up, then go back downstairs to help Jake tidy up the basement. "Man, they sure had a lot of stuff down here."

"They lived in this house for decades. You should've seen how was at the beginning. Leah would never say so, but she's been a saint dealing with everything with her parents and now this house."

"What you mean dealing with her parents?"

"Look. It's not really my story to tell. But I can say that Leah had plans to go to leave town and go to the University over in Fairview, but her parents started getting sick, so she stuck around to help look after them. Her college fund went to taking care of her parents. She wanted to leave just like you and everybody else did, but she didn't get the opportunity to."

"Man, she sure got the short stick. But it's respectable that she stayed to help her parents. They were such good people and I was truly sorry to hear when they passed."

It's frustrating to learn that Leah didn't get to pursue her dreams. The sacrifice she made is so much more than a lot of people would do, and I admire her even more. It means something when people put their family first, especially their parents.

"They are definitely going to be missed. I don't know what Leah is going to do, though. She might stay here or she might leave, but she hasn't said either way. I imagine she wants to finish up dealing with the house, and then figure things out. But I've said more than I should. You'll have to talk to her if you want to know the details."

"Got it. It's natural to be curious."

Jake laughs and punches me on the shoulder, hard enough that I grimace.

"You mean it's natural to be curious about the girl who got away. I know how you felt about her in high school. Everyone did."

"She was definitely the one who got away."

"Leah, did you really only buy a single six-pack of beer?" Jake smiles and shakes his head as he looks at Leah, and then grabs his keys. "I'll be back in ten. I'll go pick up a proper supply."

Leah and I both laugh, and the awkwardness I felt talking to her earlier begins to evaporate. She pulls her legs underneath her, while sitting at one end of the couch in the living room.

"I was really sorry to hear about your parents, Leah. What they did for Jake…that was something. Your parents were good people. I didn't hear what happened until after the funeral or I definitely would've been there. I'm sorry about that."

"Thanks, Ben." She sighs deeply and pulls at the hem of her skirt and squeezes it tightly with her fingers.

"What's next for you? Are you going to move in here?"

Leah's laugh is fast and sharp. She looks at me, her eyes blazing with fury. The change in her expression is startling.

"Did I say something wrong?"

"No, you didn't say anything wrong. You just don't know what happened." She takes the kind of breath you take when you have to count to ten so that you can calm your emotions. Obviously, this isn't going to be a happy story. "Their insurance crapped out on them, when they both got sick. I'd love to be able to keep this house, but there's no way in hell that I can afford to. I barely make enough to get by now, and there aren't any other good jobs here in town. I'd love to leave town, but I can't even afford to do that."

"That really sucks. Is there anything I can do to help?"

There is sadness and resignation in the smile Leah gives me.

"Not really, no. I mean, if you have a winning lottery ticket, I wouldn't say no to that. I'd give almost anything to be able to quit my job and to not have to work at the wood mill or the grocery store."

"What's wrong with your job?" The tone of her voice sounds alarm bells in my head. Aside from her losing this house, there's obviously a bigger problem in her life.

"It's… It's fine. It's a job and I have a bad boss. There's nothing that can really be done about it." Leah says this with a sad finality.

I take a closer look at Leah and see her hand trembling as she pushes her dark curls back from her face. Seeing her in distress like this makes me want to do anything and everything I can to help her. I can't bear to see her hurting like this, because she is such a good person. She deserves more than having her parents die, losing the house, and then having a shitty job on top of that.

"You're taking care of yourself, right? It's sounds like you got a lot going on, but you shouldn't forget to take care of yourself, too."

Leah takes a deep breath and looks away from me, the hurt written all over her face. It's frustrating see her so upset and not being able to do anything about it. I'd do anything to fix what's broken in her life.

"I do my best, Ben. But it's hard."

The silence stretches between us and before I can figure out something, anything, to do to help, my phone rings.

"Hey, Jake. You going to be much longer?"

"Ben, man. I'm sorry. I just got called into work and I can't bail on them. Can you step in and help Leah the rest of today and with the dump run tomorrow?"

"Of course. Whatever she needs, I've got it covered."

We finish our call and I hang up. I know I shouldn't be happy that Jake is tied up with work, but I am. It means I get to spend one-on-one time with Leah, and that makes me happier than I've felt in a long time. Being around her feels like something is right in the world.

I explain to Leah about Jake and do my best not to grin at the prospect of spending time with her, alone.

"Well I guess it's just you and me, then."

The smile on her plump lips makes my heart pound and my cock spasm with desire. I haven't felt this happy in a long time.

LEAH

This is been the longest day of my life. Ever since my alarm went off this morning, I've been giddy with anticipation to see Ben. Mr. Whipple senses something, because he's been more attentive than usual.

As I stand next to the copy machine, humming along to the radio as I wait for these reports to print, my body freezes when I hear the familiar breathing and smell the scent of Mr. Whipple's nasty cologne behind me. *Please let him walk away. Please let him walk away.*

"Leah. I was looking for you. I'm so happy that I found you."

I hold my breath and count to ten, to try and calm myself down. Mr. Whipple's the last thing I need right now. I've been in such a great mood and I brace myself for whatever bomb he's going to throw my way.

My printing finishes and I take as much time as I can gathering the bundles before holding them tightly against my chest. Mr. Whipple is standing closer to me than I would like when I turn around, and he's blocking the doorway to the main office. I don't know how much more of this job and him I can take, and I start considering quitting this job without a backup plan. Maybe working in the wood mill wouldn't be so bad.

But I know, deep down, that working in the wood mill really would be that bad. Maybe I could get a job waiting tables or serving drinks on the weekends, at one of the restaurants on the interstate, so I could save up some money and leave this town. The real estate agent has said it might be months before the house will sell, because this is such a small town and people aren't exactly moving here in droves. He's from the next town over, because even the idea of Mr. Whipple selling my parent's house makes my skin crawl. There's no way I want him earning a penny from the house.

If the house doesn't sell soon, I don't know what I can do. The house is still mortgaged and I can't afford to keep paying it.

"Is there something you need help with?" I mentally cross my fingers and hope that he says no. Sometimes, it's easier if he just leers at me instead of giving me more work or asking me to help him with something. The times when I have to work with him one-on-one, those are the absolute worst.

"I really like this new attitude that you have. You're so upbeat and happy." His eyes rake over my body, though a small frown appears on his face when he sees that my breasts are covered by the reports. "I would like to discuss these reports with you and to get your feedback on them. I've been thinking that we could possibly increase your responsibilities, and we could work more closely together." The way that he says *more closely* scares me.

"That sounds great, Mr. Whipple. Can we talk about that tomorrow? I want to make sure these reports are complete and ordered properly."

He takes a step closer to me and I stifle my gag reflex as his cheap cologne invades my nose.

"Today would be better, Leah. Do you really need that much more time to finish up the reports?"

"Well… I'm not exactly sure, yet. I know these are important to you and I want to make sure that everything is perfect." Sometimes appealing to his vanity is an effective way to deflect his attentions, but the way he's looking at me now, I know that today is not one of those days.

"Well if there's any way…"

I nearly cry from joy the front door to the office chimes. *Thank God. Literally saved by the bell and a customer.*

Mr. Whipple leaves the copy room before me and I stay behind for a few extra seconds, calming myself down. I wrinkle my nose at the lingering scent of his cologne and wonder how somebody who deals with the public so much is so blind to how bad he smells.

"Hello, sir. How can I help you?"

"Actually, I'm here to see Leah Burke. Is she available?"

My heart skips a beat when I hear Ben's voice. Even though he couldn't know it, he's my savior for coming in right now and interrupting Mr. Whipple.

"Hi, Ben. How are you?" I smile and then smooth my dress with one hand, while holding onto the reports in my other. The smile on Ben's face pierces deep into my soul and makes me want a future with him.

"I'm good. How are you? Are you almost ready to leave for the day?"

"Almost." I smile at him and my heart thumps in my chest.

"Leah. Can I speak with you for a minute?" The tone of Mr. Whipple's voice makes it crystal clear that this is not actually a question. I brace myself for the mini lecture that I know is coming.

"Of course, Mr. Whipple." I turn to Ben and give him a big smile. "I'll be back in just a minute. Just have a seat."

Mr. Whipple ushers me back to his office, then closes the door. The only thing keeping me from crawling out of my skin right now is the knowledge that Ben is on the other side of the door.

"Leah. What have I said about personal matters on business time?"

"I know, Mr. Whipple. I apologize. Ben's just early to pick me up from work, that's all. I'm not trying to slack off or anything." I look down at the floor because I have no interest in seeing the anger in Mr. Whipple's eyes.

"Is he a new boyfriend of yours?"

I bristle at the question, because it is so inappropriate. He's talking like it's an offense if I have a personal life.

"We're friends. Good friends." I'm not going to lie about my friendship with Ben, but I also want to be vague, because it's none of Mr. Whipple's business. "Is there anything else? I'd like to finish these before the end of the day."

I can feel Mr. Whipple's eyes boring into me, even though I'm not looking at his face. I shift my weight from foot to foot, fighting the urge to just open the door and run out of this office and never come back.

"Yes, that's fine. But don't even think about leaving one minute early."

"Of course not, Mr. Whipple."

The moment the clock strikes five, I quickly shut down my computer and lock the reports in my desk and grab my purse so that I can head out the door.

As Ben and I walk out the door, the weight of today's run-ins with Mr. Whipple lift off of me and my stress from the day fades. I look in his green eyes and feel instant happiness and comfort. Being with Ben feels righter than anything.

"I'm so glad you're here."

"Is THERE anything more that we need to pick up and bring?" Ben wipes sweat off his face as we get back into his truck. Were both panting after unloading his truck at the thrift store, but the lightness that comes with the weight of getting rid of things buoys up my mood. I'm so much closer to finishing going through everything of my parents, that that alone is a huge relief.

Nobody tells you how bad it will be to go through your parents' things once they've died. It's like you're not just grieving the death, but you're being constantly reminded about their life, and there are times when everything gets so heavy that you can't even breathe.

"No, I think that's it for today. I'd like to do more, but I just don't think I can handle it." I slump into the seats and the heaviness settles over my body. Some days, I can power through for hours and do so much. Other days, the heaviness of missing and mourning my parents overwhelms me. Some boxes hold emotional time bombs that just unleash such strong feelings that I can't do anything else for days afterward. I'm discovering things about my parents and it breaks my heart all over again, because I can't ask them about these things because they're gone.

"Hey, Leah. Are you okay? Your mood did that thing again, where it changes in an instant. It's not like you." Ben touches my arm and the kindness of the gesture unwinds something with in me and before I even realize it, tears are streaming down my face. "Leah, honey. What's wrong?"

"It's… It's hard to explain. I'm relieved that my parents aren't suffering anymore, but this is all so intense. It's like I don't have any time to breathe, especially with Mr. Whipple." I cringe as I say his name. I hate that he invades my mind so much that I can't escape him even when I'm away from the office.

"What's wrong with your boss? Is he harassing you?" The tone of Ben's voice is fierce.

"It's…fine. It's fine."

"Leah, it's not fine. I saw how he looked at you and how he talked to you. That man clearly wants you – and not as an employee. It's obvious something is wrong. Talk to me."

BEN

"Well, it's not my favorite job, no. But I don't have any other good options here in town. You know it's either work at the real estate office or work in the wood mill. I really don't like having Mr. Whipple as a boss…but what can I do?"

"Yeah, I know. It's tough. That's why I left town."

She looks at me and she asks the question I've been expecting her to ask. "But I thought you left town because you got married when you graduated?"

"It's true. Marlene didn't want to live here because she said the town was too small. I was blindly in love with her. It wasn't the only warning sign I ignored. I hadn't wanted to leave my family and friends, but I did and I've always regretted that."

"Then how come you haven't moved back?"

"I've built up a life over in Fairview. I'm settled and happy with everything else, so I just stayed. I still miss this town, but I do have to admit that it is small and there isn't a lot of opportunity here."

"Can I ask why didn't work out with you and Marlene?" Leah bites her lip and she twists her hands in her lap. As much as I hate talking about Marlene, if Leah asking means when it's I hope it does, she has to hear this and I have to know for certain that she's different than Marlene.

"There were lots of little things, but just one big thing." I pause, a sense of dread rushing through me. What if Leah isn't different than Marlene? The thought of that scares me more than I'd like to admit and it makes me realize just how invested I am in Leah. "The big thing was that she didn't want to have children. I was always clear about my desire to have a big family and she always claimed to feel the same way."

"What happened? You said 'claimed'?" Leah settles in the corner of the couch, her big eyes watching me intently.

"Well, if you asked her, Marlene would've said she wanted a lot of children. The reality was I found her birth control pills."

"I… That's just horrible. Why would somebody even lie about something like that?"

"We just weren't the right match. She wanted things that I was never going to give her, but somehow, she was hoping that I would still give them to her. I was hoping she would give me a family. We were both wrong. Divorce was the only sane option."

I watch Leah as she takes this all in, but I can't really read her reaction.

"But what about you?" I finally ask, uncomfortable with the silence and feeling so exposed to Leah. "How come you're not married and with kids? Or do you not want kids?"

"Oh, I definitely want kids! I just… I guess I haven't found the right guy. And honestly?" She looks down at her body, and then back up at me. "The guys around here just don't like my body type. They want the skinny girls who look good in bikinis in summer. It seems the only time guys talk to me is if they're drunk or feeling desperate. And I'm not that desperate."

"That's absolutely ludicrous, Leah. You're fucking gorgeous and anyone who tries to tell you differently is blind or insane." I look at her curvy body and despite the serious conversation we're having, a fire of lust flares in me. She has a kind of body that I dream about going to bed with night and waking up next to every morning, and touching every chance that I have. She's goddamn perfect.

"I… Thanks. But you don't have to be nice to me."

"Leah. I'm serious. I was always attracted to you, and now that you're growing up? You're sexy as fuck. Do you really not see that?" It's hard even wrap my mind around the idea that she doesn't see herself as attractive. I get that some guys like the thin girls, but I've always liked girls I had a little extra meat on their bones. Their curves are sexy and making love with a curvy girl is just the best thing in the world.

"I guess so? I mean, sure I think I'm attractive, but it's hard to feel that way when you're the last girl that somebody asks out on a date or when guys just ignore you. I always end up feeling invisible, like I'm not worth seeing." She wraps her arms tightly around her chest and looks directly at the ground, her body rigid.

Anger rises up in me that Leah has had to endure this. At the same time, I'm overjoyed that she's single. I need her in my life more than anything. I move next to her on the couch and put my hand on her arm gently.

"You're not invisible, Leah. I see you." I wait for her to look at me, and then I lean in and do what I've been wanting to do since I first saw her again. I kiss her luscious lips and revel in the feeling of finally getting a taste of what I've always wanted. Her body relaxes and she turns toward me, and our kiss deepens. I wrap my arms around her and shudder at how good this feels, how beyond perfect Leah is.

"Oh…"

I push her curly hair back from her face so that I can see her more clearly.

"I've wanted to kiss you like that for a very long time."

"Was that what you expected?" A smile plays on her lips and my cock tightens even more as I look at her. She's playful and intelligent, and I love it.

"I'm not sure," I tease, running my fingers down her neck and shoulder and slipping them under the edge of her blouse and caressing her silky skin. "I think I need to investigate further. Do you have any objections to this?"

Leah giggles and shakes her head. She leans toward me and I groan. Our kiss is deeper and it goes straight to my cock. The way she moans into my mouth, I know that she wants me just as badly as I need her.

I'm not leaving this town without her.

LEAH

"Oh my God, Annie! It was so unexpected!" I'm sitting in the break room in the office, trying to talk as quietly as possible into my cell phone so that I'm not overheard. It's my lunch break and I can talk to whomever I want on my own time and on my own phone, but I certainly don't want Mr. Whipple to overhear any of this. It's not his business.

"But are you happy?"

"I am. I liked him so much in high school, but he was older and then he got involved with that Marlene girl."

"Yeah, I heard about that. What happened with them? I thought they got married."

"It just didn't work out. They got divorced." As much as I love my best friend, I'm not going to air Ben's laundry with her.

"But he's single and available now, right?"

"One hundred percent. I'm certain." I close my eyes and smile as I recall how we made out the other night. He had to go home for a couple of days, but promised to come back today and I've been counting every minute until today. "There's something here. He's the one."

Annie laughs, but I know it's a happy laugh. "Girl, I hope so. You deserve happiness more than anybody I know."

"Thanks. This just feels different, you know? It feels right."

"Sure do. Look, I gotta run. We'll talk soon, alright? I want to hear more about this."

I TAKE a break and walk around the house. It takes my breath away to see how much progress we've all made. Especially with Ben being able to help out, things have moved so much faster than I expected. Before even Jake came to help, I put aside the important things like the photo albums and their marriage certificate, and little things like my mom's favorite salt and pepper shakers, my dad's toolbox, and other things I'm particularly attached to. Dad was always fixing things and teaching me how to fix things, and now I'll remember him every time I need a wrench or a hammer. I'm sentimental, but it's so weird that I don't want to keep everything of theirs. Though I know a lot of that is because I'll be lucky to afford a small apartment and I simply won't have the space. Maybe if I had the money to buy this house and keep living here, but I don't and so I can't.

The progress that we've made here feels good, but seeing the rooms empty is also bittersweet. It's so strange to sort through and dispose of somebody else's life, especially for your parents. Emotions engulf me and I make my way back to the living room and sit down heavily on the couch. I run my hands against the knees of my jeans, willing myself to keep it together and not start crying. My emotions rise up at the most unexpected times. Sometimes what I'm going through things that I feel like I should be emotional about, the motion stone calm. But then I might go to the kitchen and pick up a fork, and then I see it was my mom's favorite fork, and then I absolutely lose it.

"Hey, Leah. Where are you?"

I smile at the sound of Ben's voice and then smile wider as he walks into the living room.

"Oh! I'm glad I found you. Have you seen this box of letters?" He walks over to me, a large and worn shoebox under his arm.

"I don't think so. It sure looks dusty."

"It definitely is, but I wiped it down as much and as carefully as I could. Here."

Ben gives me the box and put it on my lap. I look at the faded blue paper of the box and run my hands over it. I take a deep breath and carefully lift the lid off of the box.

"Oh, wow." My mouth falls open as I look at a box filled with letters. I pull a few out and I recognize both my mom's and my dad's handwriting. When I look at the postmarks, I realize that Ben is just found the letters and my parents into each other before they got married.

I open one of the letters and skim the contents, and my eyes filled with tears. *There is something about you that is so special, I can't keep away.* My father's letters to my mother have a romantic eloquence that I didn't know that he had. When I open one of hers, her letters are no less affectionate, but there's a restraint to them. I carefully put the letter back in its envelope and then press it to my chest.

"These are so special. I don't know how I missed this box. I'm so thankful that you found it, Ben. Thank you so much."

"It was hidden in the back of the kitchen, behind a bunch of old pots and pans. I'm not surprised you never saw it before." Ben's voice is gentle and it makes me care for him even more, that he can see me be emotional and not close off or make fun of me. I can trust him.

I join Ben in clearing up the rest of the kitchen and we work together in a companionable silence. I've delayed working on the kitchen, because we made so many family meals and good memories here. When the last of the old pots and pans and dishes are boxed up and ready to go to the thrift store, we grab a couple of beers from the refrigerator and go relax on the couch as we wait for Jake to finish upstairs.

"I'm so thankful that you're here, Ben. You've helped so much."

"If you need help with anything, Leah, even aside from this house, all you have to do is ask. I will always be here for you and I will do anything I can to help you."

"Know of any good jobs?" I ask wistfully, trying to laugh and shake off the feelings that I have about my job. "Sorry. That was a bad attempt at a joke."

"There are lots of jobs in Fairview. Have you ever considered moving?"

I look at Ben quickly and my mind races at the possibilities – not just of a new, better job, but of also being closer to him. I've avoided thinking about what happens when he goes back home.

"It's tempting, Ben. You have no idea."

"I think I have an idea. I don't know if you realize how happy it would make me, too, if you were in Fairview. I wouldn't let anything ever come between us. Do you realize how much I care for you?"

My heart expands and I realize that in the middle of the most difficult thing I've ever faced, I've found something special with Ben. The kiss wasn't a fluke and what I felt was real. *Is* real. I put my bottle of beer down and move so that I'm sitting next to Ben, our legs touching.

"I think I'd like to hear more about this." I smile at Ben, then lean over and kiss him on the lips. Ben kisses me back and I feel happier than I have in months. For once, it feels like things are going my way.

"Was that enough? Because I can talk about this all night long, if you like."

"Yes, please."

The moment that Ben's lips meet mine again, there's a banging at the front door.

"Are you expecting anyone?" Ben asks, his green eyes suddenly alert.

"No, I'm not," I say as we walk to the front door.

I open the door and my heart sinks.

BEN

The way Leah's face crumples and falls when her boss appears at her front door, something shifts deep inside of me and I move to stand in front of her.

"Why are you here?" I stare at her boss, disgusted that he's shown up here. I've seen the way this jackass looks and talks to Leah, and my fists clench and ache to punch him in the nose. He blinks quickly and squints his eyes at me, but doesn't talk to me directly.

"Leah. If I can have a word?" He talks to her like he owns her and I'm not standing in front of Leah.

"Do you need something, Mr. Whipple?" Leah thrusts her chin forward, but her voice trembles. When she grabs my hand with hers, she squeezes so tightly that it hurts. "We can talk here. Ben can hear whatever it is you have to say. I trust him completely."

Mr. Whipple shifts the weight of his feet and looks surprised. I'm guessing that Leah always goes along with whatever he says, which makes sense given how she's described the lack of job opportunities here in town. I'm so proud of her for challenging him.

"Well, I came to ask if you are ready to start talking about putting this house on the market. It's no secret that you have to sell, and you know that I know the local real estate markets. I'll forgive you to talking to a different agent." He laughs smugly and tension coils in my body.

"Mr. Whipple. I've already talked to another agent. I don't need your opinion or your help."

I put my arm around Leah shoulder and pull her tightly to me. Leah is mine.

"You know how fast the things move around here, despite this being a small town. And this house," he says moving his hand in a large gesture and trying to lean in and look around the house. "This house is in a prime location and I know I can sell it in an instant. Why don't you just let me come in and have a look around."

"I don't think so." Leah's voice is audibly shaking now and a rage courses through my veins.

Mr. Whipple ignores her and steps into the house. I put my hand on his chest and stare at him as he glares at me with his small, beady eyes.

"Just what do you think you're doing?" The color of embarrassment and anger rises in his face.

"Leah did not invite you in, so you are not invited. Is that clear?" My body is humming with adrenaline and my fingers are twitching. This guy is a piece of work in the worst possible way and it makes me angry that he's Leah's boss.

"Get out of my way. I don't know who you think you are, but you have no idea who I am." He pushes my arm, unable to move me, then sidesteps my arm and steps into the house.

The world slows for a moment and then my fist is launching and it hits him square in the middle of his face. The distinct crunch of his nose breaking is the only sound.

"She said no. Now leave before that happens again."

He looks at me, his eyes wild as he holds his hands to his nose to try and stop the bleeding. He looks from me to Leah and back to me. Wisely, he turns and walks down the pathway to the sidewalk.

My hand shakes as I close the door. Adrenaline is still flooding through my system. I'm not afraid to get into fights and I will always defend the people who are important to me, but the honest truth is that I don't like to fight. But there's something satisfying about a physical altercation and establishing dominance. And some weaselly man in a cheap suit is not dominant to me.

I turn to Leah, not sure what to expect from her. Her eyes are wide as she looks at me.

"I shouldn't have done that. I…"

"It's… I don't want to say it's okay, but… It's not the end of the world? Though I have to admit I'm a bit scared to go into work tomorrow, because I know he'll make my life hell. He's a petty man and he knows how hard jobs are to come by unless there at the mill."

"Then quit. I was serious when I asked you to come to Fairview. There are so many more jobs there and I can take care of you and look out for you." More than anything, I want to save her from this life that is causing her nothing by heartache and despair. I want give her a life she loves, and I want to love her and be loved by her.

"Are you serious?" Her voice is soft as she looks up at me.

"I am absolutely serious, Leah. Let's sit down and talk."

I guide her back into the living room and we sit back down on the couch. I hold her hands in mine and carefully watch her face.

"That would be a really big step."

"It would be. But Leah, you know it's the right decision." I take a deep breath and steady my nerves. No one tells you just how difficult it will be when you're going to lay your heart on the table in front of the woman you love. "It's impossible to deny that there is something between us, something unbreakable. I know beyond a shadow of a doubt that you're the woman for me. I know you and I love you."

I look at Leah and watch her reaction, and I realize I've never felt this scared. My life is riding on her answer. As her lips form into a smile, it feels better than winning the lottery. Having all the money in the world would mean nothing if I didn't have Leah.

"You really feel that way about me?" Leah reaches up and runs her hand along my jaw.

"I do, Leah. I liked you when we were younger and seeing you again? It makes me realize that I was a fool for ever letting you go, back then. I know beyond a shadow of a doubt that you are the only woman I will ever love."

"I…" Leah's mouth opens and closes as she struggles for words. Her voice is quiet, yet firm when she finally speaks. "Yes! I'll do it. I love you, too!"

"Sweetheart, I'm so glad to hear you say that. I don't know what I would've done if you would said no."

"Do you want to know a secret?" She pauses and bites her lip. After I nod my head, she continues. "I feel the same way about you. I liked you so much in high school and it terrified me. When I saw you again the other day, all of those emotions came rushing back. And spending time with you has only shown me that everything I believed to be true about you in high school, that it was true and is still true. You are the only man for me."

Leah kisses me with her full lips and my body is hungry to make love to Leah.

"Words aren't enough to tell you how happy you make me, Leah. But there's something that we need to do. Right now."

LEAH

"This is the best day," I say, reaching over and running my fingers through Ben's light hair. I want to be as close to him as possible. I want to give him what I've been saving for someone special.

"It's about to get a lot better."

"Oh! I can finally tell Mr. Whipple that I quit! I didn't think this day could be any better, but it is!" A wave of excitement rushes over me and I giggle uncontrollably. "Oh my God! I am so not going to miss that job."

"I want you to have the best life possible, Leah. I will do everything in my power to make you and keep you happy."

"You really are wonderful, you know." I squeeze his hand tightly and feels so thankful that he loves me, too.

"You're not so bad yourself," he teases, squeezing my hand back. "But don't tell my friends that," he laughs. "I wouldn't hear the end of it if they knew I was really a softie."

"Don't worry, Ben. Your secret is safe with me." I love that he's different with me, that I brought out this side of him that he doesn't share with anyone else. He makes me feel so special, that it takes my breath away. Now that he's in my life, I can't imagine how I ever made it this far without him. He's the piece of me that I didn't even realize existed.

"Now come with me. There's one room in this house I haven't seen yet, and I want to."

"I might have guessed that's where you want to go." I smile and take his hand, and lead him upstairs and to my bedroom. I've always planned it would be the last room I deal with, since it's mine.

"It's a nice room. I can't wait to show you my bedroom." Ben comes over to me and holds my face as he kisses me. "What's important is that I make love to you and show you just how much I love you."

I return his kiss, the passion I feel blinding me to anything else but Ben. His hands pull at my clothes and bolts of erotic electricity shock me as his hands touch my bare skin. Shivers of excitement run through me, especially as I realize I'm not scared for him to see me naked. I've always been scared to let a man see me naked, but I trust Ben. He's proven that he loves me and loves my body, just as it is.

Ben's lips on mine, he moves us over to the bed and I laugh into our kiss as we fall through the air and onto my soft bed.

"I'm so ready for this. For you." My breathing is fast and jagged as we pause long enough for Ben to stand back up and take off his clothes. "Oh, wow. You're gorgeous."

I bite my lip as I stare at his perfect body. Narrow waist, broad shoulders, more muscles than I can possibly count. He looks sexier than a movie star and I have to pinch myself to remind myself that he's real, that what we have is real. Finding Ben was like winning the lottery for love, only our love will become richer than money could ever make us.

"You're gorgeous, too, you know," Ben says, climbing into my bed and pressing his body against mine. He moves his hand over my body, from my legs to my stomach, before lingering his touch on my breasts. "Your body is perfect."

"It's not too…too much for you?" I ask, a wave of insecurity suddenly crashing over me.

"Too much? Oh hello no. You are gorgeous exactly how you are. I wouldn't have you any other way, than how you are now or how you want to be in the future. My love is for you and I will always love your body, too. These things are not separate."

"Oh, Ben." Tears of happiness prick at my eyes, and then we're kissing again, but it's fierce this time. It's like we can't get close enough, can't taste each other enough. My skin burns with heat and a different fire builds inside of me, making me squirm. "I need you," I whisper.

"I want you on top. I want to watch you as you begin learning how wonderful sex is," Ben says. His green eyes are filled with love and tenderness, and they erase any traces of self-consciousness I still have.

"But... I... This is my first time. I don't know how to do anything." I look at Ben, feeling so uncertain.

"Trust your body, Leah. I want to touch every part of your body, always." Ben caresses me as I move myself over his hips. "Just do what comes naturally, at the pace it feels natural for you. Don't worry about me."

I feel Ben's cock bumps against my core and I suddenly understand what he means. My body grinds down against his cock, hungry for it. Ben holds his cock for me, and I slide onto him, crying out from how good it feels. He's so big, but my body takes over and my hips move over him, taking him a little bit deeper each time.

"Oh, God. You feel so amazing!" Ben groans as his body moves beneath me. His hands are gripping onto my hips, and I like how it feels. He moves one of his hands around my back and pulls me so that we're chest to chest.

"This... Oh! Yes, right there!" My body is lit up from inside, a pleasure building up inside of me that is bigger than anything I've felt before. It feels as big as my love for Ben, and it takes my breath away. I don't know how I can feel so much without it exploding from it all.

Ben claims my mouth in a hot kiss and wraps his arms around me and holds me so tightly. I grind down on to him, my core hot with desire and a blinding need to have him deep inside of me. Ben thrusts up into me and something otherworldly takes us both over. We're kissing and touching our bodies are moving together faster and faster.

"Oh my God! I think I'm about to come!" What we're doing with our bodies feels nothing like how my body does when I masturbate. This is so much more powerful and addictive.

"Yes, baby! Come on my cock! Give yourself over to me!" Then wraps his lips and tongue around one of my nipples and sucks so hard that I scream out in pleasure. My hips grind on his cock faster and faster and harder, my body aching as it works to push itself over the edge.

And then I'm coming, and my juices are flowing over and as my body shakes and pushes down, hungry for even more.

"That was amazing!" I pant, slowly moving my hips over Ben. I feel so sensitive and he is so hard inside of me, that I don't know if I need a break. "I want more. I want you to feel as good as I do."

Ben makes a sound like a growl and wraps his arms around me, and flips me over so that I'm on my back.

"Let me know if this too much for you," Ben says as his hips start plunging his cock deep inside of me, faster and faster. I spread my legs as wide as I can and push my hips up to meet his thrusts.

"Give me more, then. Please!" There's a new hunger inside of me and it's fueled by my love for Ben and how making love with him feels. I never imagined that sex could feel like this, but I know that this is more than just sex… It's a pure expression of our love.

Ben lowers himself to me and kisses me deeply as his body shakes and he plunges deep into my core. I wrap my arms around him and hold him so tightly.

"You are so beautiful when you come, Leah. You have no idea." Ben gently puts his hands on the side of my face and pulls my mouth to him and gives me and tender kiss. As we lay in bed together, his hands never leave my body.

"That tickles!" I wiggle around in bed as Ben starts intentionally tickling the curve of my hips.

"I didn't know you were ticklish." Ben's lips twitch devilishly as he puts a leg over mine and starts tickling me in earnest.

"Neither did I! Stop, please!" I'm laughing and I love this moment with Ben, but the sensitivity of my skin right now is astounding. "Thanks," I say, grabbing at his hand and holding it in mine.

"There is a lot to learn about you, my darling Leah."

"And we have a whole lifetime for that, Ben. I love you so much that it feels like I'm going to burst. You're the best thing that's ever happened to me." Tears of happiness well up and Ben kisses them away from my eyes.

"You're the most important part of my life, Leah. I will always love you and always take care of you. You are mine."

EPILOGUE

"Are you ready yet?" Ben calls up the stairs to me and I can tell he's impatient to go to dinner.

"I'm coming, Ben!" I called him, checking my makeup and hair one final time, to make sure it's perfect. Satisfied with how I look, I head downstairs to meet Ben.

"That's what you said an hour ago," he teases, fox-whistling at me as I come down the stairs. "You look fucking amazing and that dress, Leah."

"And I hope to be saying that again after dinner, too." I give Ben a quick kiss on the lips, then pull back when he starts to deepen the kiss. "You're going to make us late for dinner," I tease, putting my arm through his.

Everything has changed so much in the last year with Ben. Every minute of every hour is better and better.

Every love song on the radio describes only a tiny percentage of how I feel for him. I'm doing my best to hide it, but I have a special surprise for Ben tonight. I've been bursting with the news for days now, but I wanted to save it for tonight so that our anniversary can be even more special.

"Would you care for dessert?" The waiter asks, looking from me to Ben and back to me. I look over the menu and I can't decide between the molten chocolate cake or the mixed berry cobbler.

"Can you give us a few minutes to decide?" Ben asks, pulling the dessert menu for my hands as the waiter walks away.

"Do you want to choose?" Ben always lets me choose, because he's not much of a dessert person. He's happy to have one or two bites of whatever I order. We've been together a year now and he still won't tell me if he has a favorite dessert, always saying that's a taste of what I have is more than enough for him.

"Leah, my love. Happy anniversary. I've already chosen." I look at Ben and smile, because he looks amazing in his dress shirt and sport jacket. He refuses to wear a tie, but he still looks perfect.

"Is everything okay? You look so serious."

"Leah, I love you more than life itself. If you would choose me to be your husband, it would make me happier than any man in the world."

I've known this was coming, because we've talked about getting married, but my emotions at him finally popping the question overwhelm me. He reaches into the pocket of his jacket and pulls out a beautiful blue velvet box. I gasp when he opens it and I see the prettiest, most sparkling diamond ring that I've ever seen.

"Oh, Ben! Yes! You make me the happiest woman in the world. There's nothing more that I want, but to spend the rest of my life with you, building a family together. I will be honored to be your wife."

Tears of joy fall from my eyes as Ben slides the ring on my finger, his hands trembling. As we kiss, couples at the tables around us start cheering and clapping.

"I totally forgot anybody else was here," I whisper into Ben's ear and giggle, hugging him tightly.

"You're the only person in the world that matters. Do you want dessert or something else?"

"Ben, what I really want is to go home with you and have dessert in bed." I tease, lowering my hand under the tablecloth and stroking the inside of Ben's thigh. "But I have some news of my own."

"Oh?" Then places his hand on mine and moves its so that my fingers are stroking his rock-hard cock.

"Well," I pick up one his hands and place it on my stomach. "About that family we were talking about? We've already started one."

Everything freezes in that moment. Ben and I share a look that conveys emotions that there aren't even words for. His mouth forms in an O and then he blinks rapidly, looking from my face down to my stomach and back to my face again.

"I'm going to be a dad? I'm going to be a dad!" Ben kisses me hard, taking my breath away, and then jumps up and pumps his arm and dances around like he's just won the lottery. He reaches for my hands and pulls me up so that I'm standing with him, and then he hugs me so tightly I feel like my ribs are going to break. "I'm going to be a dad!"

By now, the whole restaurant is clapping and cheering for us. Ben kisses me again, and I give everything to him in the kiss that I give back to him. We're not for big public displays of affection, but right now, I don't care. We are the happiest couple of the world and who cares if everyone sees it.

The owner of the restaurant comes up to us and claps bend on the back.

"Congratulations, you two! Dinner is my treat tonight. Consider it my engagement gift to one of my favorite couples."

"Thank you so much, Roberto," I say, reaching out and touching his arm. The light from the restaurant hits my ring and sparkles fly through the air.

"I appreciate it, my friend. You know this is our favorite restaurant. And as much as I'd love to stay for desserts, I need to take my future wife home right now."

Roberto winks at both of us and nods his head. I pick up my purse and smile at everyone as we leave the restaurant.

At every stop light, the cars behind us have to honk at us when the light turns green, because Ben and I can take our hands off of each other and we're making out like horny teenagers.

"I am proud that you will be my wife, Leah. You are more than I ever hoped to find in a woman."

I run my hand along Ben's jaw, the purest form of happiness filling me up. I still have to pinch myself all the time, because I don't know how I got so lucky.

"I never imagined that happiness can feel like this." I say, reaching out and touching Ben's chest, "or like this," I say, placing my hand on my stomach. "Every day is brighter and more fulfilling than the day before, with you. I feel safe with you and loved beyond comprehension, and that is so much more than I ever dreamed to have. You are my heart and soul. I will love you forever."

Ben blinks rapidly and swipes his hand across his eyes. He has a big, gruff exterior, but he's a total softie inside and not afraid to show me his emotions, and that makes me love him even more. We both start laughing as yet another car honks at us because we've missed the light turning green.

"I think you need to put both hands on the wheel and drive us home as fast as legally possible," I tease.

Ben laughs and does just that. His strong fingers wrap around the steering wheel and I can see them flexing as he fights the urge to touch me again. I've never been touched so much in my life as I have in the past year with Ben. There is no doubting the love that he has for me and shows me throughout every day that we're together.

"It kills me to not touch you, Leah. You know that, right?"

"I do, my love, I do. But the sooner we're home," I say, reaching over and quickly tickling the top of his leg with my fingers, "the sooner we can get into bed."

"I'm looking forward to a lifetime with you."

And with that, he floors the accelerator and drives his home in record speed.

CHASING HER CURVES

JUSTINE

The sun feels good as I walk through the park and search for an empty picnic bench. The park is always surprisingly busy on weekdays, with more than just moms bringing their kids to the playground.

"Mind if I join you?"

I follow the sound of a deep male voice and find myself looking at a muscular wall of man. His arms are covered in tattoos and he has that loose-limbed look about him that makes him look like he's ready for something physical, whether it's a fight or sex. My body heats up as I ogle his body and then look up to his chiseled face. I can hear my father's voice telling me this man is no good, that he would do nothing but break my heart and break the law.

LANA LOVE

But he's the kind of man that I find sexier than anyone. I'm still a virgin, but there's something about this man that makes me want to give him everything. There's just something about a bad boy who rides a motorcycle and isn't afraid to get dirty or criminal, that just sets something deep inside of my body purring. My dad wants me to be a good girl – and I am a good girl – but after just a glimpse of this man, I want to be the baddest girl ever and break all the rules with him.

"Sure. Just don't try any funny business," I laugh, gesturing toward the other side of the table with my hand. I yearn for him to sit next to me, but I know that's a spectacularly bad decision. There's no way I could resist touching his muscles and tracing my fingertips over his tattoos.

"You got some big boyfriend I should know about?" The man laughs. I like that he picks up on my sense of humor and that I'm not left explaining my joke.

"No. No boyfriend. But my dad's the chief of police."

The man looks at me steadily, clearly uncertain as to whether or not I'm still joking. I smile at him and then take a bite of my sandwich and look over to some kids playing in the field next to us.

"Then no funny business it is. My name's Harley."

I laugh so hard that I nearly choke on my sandwich. I wipe my mouth with my napkin and then take a long drink of water to clear my throat.

"You have got to be kidding. Are you really a biker with the name Harley?"

"That is true."

"Is that your real name?" The coincidence seems too much. "What are the odds of somebody named Harley grows up and becomes a motorcycle guy?"

"How do you know I'm a motorcycle guy? You think because I have tattoos that it means I ride a bike?"

"You have the walk and the look. And the jacket," I say, looking at his well-worn and custom jacket. I know exactly what and who I'm looking at.

"And just how do you know how a biker walks and looks?" Harley openly looks at as much of me as he can see above the picnic table. I watch him nod his head as he takes in my cotton blouse and cardigan. If anything, I look like a grade-school teacher or librarian, not someone who knows anything about men like him.

"I just know things. And remember, dad is the chief of police?"

Harley rolls his green eyes at me and laughs. You'd think that guys would be turned off when I tell them that my dad is the chief of police, but men either don't believe me or they take it as a personal challenge. Harley clearly doesn't believe me.

"Right. So, don't you have a job? How is it that you're sitting in a park in the middle of the day?"

"I work in retail and my shift doesn't start until the afternoon. Also, I need to take my dad his lunch."

Harley raises his eyebrow at me. "Why can't your dad get his own lunch?"

I sigh and look away from Harley, a pang of sadness coming over me.

"If I don't bring my dad lunch, he doesn't eat. And if he doesn't eat, then he gets difficult. Ever since my mom died, he's had a really hard time. If he could live on just fast food, he would. But I like my dad and I don't want him to have a heart attack," I reach into my bag and pull up the lunch that I bought for my dad and hold it up, "so I bring my dad lunch when I can. I don't want to lose him, too."

"I'm sorry to hear about your mother. It's sounds like you were close?" Harley's voice softens and it takes me by surprise, because it sounds like he genuinely cares.

I take a long look at Harley, a little bit surprised at how he's such a contradiction. He has such a tough exterior, but he seems genuinely kind. I know that you shouldn't judge people by how they look, but I'm still surprised. My dad says that a person's exterior more often than not matches their interior.

"Yes. I loved her more than anything. Pardon my language, but fuck cancer."

Harley looks away from me and when he looks back to me, there is a tenderness in his eyes. How is it that a hulking man, dressed in leathers, cares so much about how I feel? We're nothing but strangers to each other.

"No need to apologize… Hey, you haven't told your name."

I smile and get up from the picnic table. "It was nice to meet you Harley, you're not what I expected. I hope you have a good afternoon."

Harley looks at me, his mouth hanging open. He certainly not the type of man that I imagine other girls walk away from. God's honest truth, it's not what I want, either. But my dad would kill me if I did more than say hello to a man like Harley. I know my dad doesn't control me, but I don't want to disappoint him, ever.

It takes every ounce of willpower that I have, and then some, not to look back over my shoulder and see if Harley's watching me, or to do what I really want, which is to turn around and go back to him.

"I don't know why you keep doing this," my dad says, sighing as he opens the bag of food I brought him.

"I do it because I love you, dad, and because I know what you eat if I don't."

"Thank you, Justine." He pulls the sandwich out of the bag and smiles when he peeks inside the paper wrapping. "Your mom used to make the best tuna salad sandwich."

"I remember, dad. I've been scouring the city to find a place that makes one half as good as mom did. I think this one might be close."

My dad walks over to me and wraps his arms around me and gives me a fierce hug. I feel his Kevlar vest under his shirt, and I close my eyes and say a silent prayer for my dad. He doesn't have to go out in the field often, but I always get scared when he does. And if he's wearing that vest today, then he must be going out.

"You be safe, dad, okay?" I try and steady my voice as I look at him. I don't know what I would do without him.

"Chief Harwell? Your next appointment is here." His assistant stands at the door, looking at my dad expectantly. My dad looks at him and then down to the sandwich on his desk.

"Two minutes, Gardner." My dad says, circling around his desk, then taking two big bites of the sandwich before he's even sat down.

"This is why I bring you lunch," I say, laughing as I watch him wolf the sandwich down. "It's like you told me when I was a kid. To do good work, you have to have a full stomach."

My dad rolls his eyes and smiles, wiping the corners of his mouth with a napkin.

"Anything in my teeth?" He asks, standing up and walking me to his office door. My dad stands up straight and pushes out his chest in an exaggerated way, making me laugh.

"Nope. It's all clear. I'll let you get on with your meeting. I need to go to work anyway." I give my dad another hug and kiss him on the cheek, and then stand to the side as he opens the door for me.

"You?"

My insides go molten as I hear the voice that I didn't want to walk away from half an hour ago.

"Harley? What are you doing here?" My mind spins and races as to what it means that he has an appointment with my dad. A complex set of emotions crosses Harley's eyes as he looks from me to my dad, and then back to me.

"I thought you were joking about your dad."

HARLEY

"How do you know my daughter?" Chief Harwell demands, sitting down heavily behind his desk. He fixes me with a laser gaze, silent.

It's none of your damn business. Of course, I can't say that to the man who may very well control how I spend the next several years of my life.

"We just met in the park, for a few minutes. It's nothing."

I wanted it to be something, but life isn't a fairytale or opposites work out. And if there were ever two more opposite people, it would be this girl, Justine, and me.

I maintain eye contact with Chief Harwell. Fuck if I'm going to back down. Justine has nothing to do with this right here and her dad knows it. I can understand the straitlaced father not wanting his sweet daughter to date a man with my history, but that's not why I'm here. I don't ask for permission.

"You would do well to forget my daughter. I don't know what you think or what happened, but she's totally off limits."

Like I'm going to let a police officer tell me what to do.

"Sure," I say, trying to brush off his demand as if it meant nothing to me. The reality is it's like throwing a red flag in front of the bull. You tell me not to do something and I'm damn well going to turn around and do it.

"Back to the matter at hand. You know why you're here. I need you to tell me why you are wiring money to Albania."

I stare back at Chief Harwell.

"Is it a crime to send money to Albania?" I challenge. I know I haven't broken any laws and it's bullshit I was called in to talk to the chief of police.

"No, it's not. But when you send money to someone that the feds are investigating for human trafficking, questions are raised."

"Then why am I talking to you instead of the feds?"

Chief Harwell stares at me and takes a deep breath.

"You're talking with me because if they pull you in, it's not for a friendly chat. And this, here," he says, waving his hand over his desk, "is supposed to be a friendly chat. So how about being friendly?"

I stare back at Chief Harwell, trying to decide if I tell him what he wants to know. I know he knows I have a record and a past. I also know that he knows that I haven't been on the radar of the police in a long time. It's been years since I was arrested or doing anything worth being arrested for.

"No," I say, standing up. "That's going to be a no. I'm sure you've looked at my record, so it will come as no surprise to you to learn I don't trust the cops."

"Then why'd you come in?"

"It wasn't clear what you knew or what you thought I did. Now, I know that you're in the dark, and that's fine with me. Have a good day." I turn and walk out before he can try and push me any further. I'm goddamn doing what he can't – ain't no way I'm going to help a cop out. Because if I told him what I'm doing, then he *will* see that some things I do are outside the law.

Whether he knows it or not, the world is a better place when I break the law, and he needs more people like me.

It's only after I've been riding for an hour that my emotions begin to calm. Roaring down the highway, my chopper purring like the beautiful machine she is – there's nothing that can calm me down like that.

There's a deeper desire within me to just keep on riding and leave Chief Harwell and his suspicions behind me. But that would mean leaving my brothers in arms and that's not something that I can do.

Fuck.

I knew it was only a matter of time before law enforcement came sniffing. We're only doing what they can't.

Leaving town would also mean never seeing Justine again, and that is out of the question. Meeting her was a stroke of luck on my part. She's clearly a very special woman and I'm not about to let her get away. Justine has that magic that I've looked for in a woman for myself, for years. Not to mention, the memory of her soft curves makes me hard as fuck. She has the kind of demure sexiness that I know is just a mask for a woman who is a wildcat in bed.

I've always found that the women who are the quietest to be the sexiest women of all. Give me a woman who looks like a grade school teacher or a librarian, and I go weak in my fucking knees.

Reluctantly, I take the off ramp and then turn around and head back to town.

I don't care what it takes or what kind of punishment her father is going to dole out to me, but I'm going back for Justine and I'm going to claim her for myself.

JUSTINE

"Thanks, Justine." My dad takes the meal from me and gives me a big hug. "I can't talk right now, but we'll talk later. Oh, and one more thing. You haven't seen the biker again, have you?"

The look on my dad's face makes it clear exactly how he feels about Harley. If he could, my dad would protect me from anything bad in the world and also make sure that no man ever got close to me.

"No, I haven't."

"Good. Keep it that way." I watch my dad as he walks through the precinct, and then I turn to leave.

Though if I'm honest with myself, I know that I shouldn't even think about him. Bad boys are sexy, but seeing Harley waiting to talk to my dad? That was a little bit too much for me. I've grown up hearing about criminals and what they do and how they treat women, and that's not something that I want for myself and it's not something I want for the children that I plan on having. I need a man who loves me and protects me, and who won't jack me around or end up in prison for years on end.

Still, no matter what I do, I can't stop thinking about Harley. The way he was so kind and thoughtful with me doesn't match how I thought someone in a motorcycle club would be like. Even with his leather jacket on, tattoos on his chest…I've been driving myself to distraction at night, imagining how far his tattoos go down his chest and his stomach. I want to lick his tattoos.

I know my dad means well for me, but the desire to spread my wings and do things that I've been told not to…it's powerful. I want to date the bad boy and see what that's like. I'm tired of being the good girl that my dad and everyone else thinks I should be. My dad warns me about danger, but I want to taste it.

I walk to the park so that I can sit in the sun before going to work at the department store, my mind drifting back to Harley. There are clouds scudding across the sky, but the sun is winning and spreading warmth everywhere. I sit down at my favorite picnic table and close my eyes, relishing the hot warmth of the sun on my face. In my fantasy, he shows up when I open my eyes.

"Well look at you, you pretty little thing. Sitting here all by yourself. Don't you know that's dangerous, little girl?"

My body goes into instant alert mode and I open my eyes to see a greasy looking guy standing in front of me. I can't tell if he's homeless or if he's a junkie.

"Keep on moving. I'm not interested." I work to keep my voice steady and to hide how fast my heart is racing. It's the middle of the day, in the middle of the park, but for once there aren't that many people around.

The sound of the guy's laughing makes my skin crawl.

"Oh, little girl. I'm interested." He towers over me and I just know that this is going to end badly.

I discreetly take my phone out of my skirt pocket and quickly glance down as I unlock it, then I try to tap into my address book so that I can call my dad. He's taught me better than to try and fight someone like this guy. In fact, he's told me to just give whatever somebody likes this wants, and not to try and fight.

"And what I'm really interested in, little girl, is that shiny little phone of yours. So just hand it over and this doesn't have to get mean." He leans even closer to me and I wince at the center of his stale breath.

"I don't think so. My father is the chief of police, just so you know." I really am feeling more than a little bit scared right now and I wrap my fingers tightly around my phone. I try to tap to make a call, but the guy quickly snatches my phone out of my hand.

Fuck! I know my dad says to give a thief whatever they want, but my phone has my life in it. I don't want to let it go!

"And where is your daddy now, little girl? Doesn't matter who he is if he isn't here to protect you."

"Give it back!"

"You got something else to give me, instead, little girl?" The guy leers at me and I instinctively lean away from him.

I shake my head, lacking confidence and how my voice would sound if I tried to talk. My emotions and adrenaline are surging, and I hate that I feel like I'm about to start crying. I want to be a bad ass, but I don't know how.

"Please, can I have it back?" I plead with the thief. Deep down, I know that it's futile to do this, but I can't stop myself.

"Is there a problem here?" A familiar voice says from behind me.

I can't be that lucky, can I?

Harley comes into view and words can't express how grateful I am to see him. His face is a fearsome mask and I can see him flexing his arm muscles.

"No, man. Nothing to see here. I'm just enjoying my brand-new phone."

Harley looks at me and I look up at him. I try to tell him everything with my eyes and the way he squints at me and then turns back to the thief, I'm sure he understands.

"Let me see the phone." His voice is an unwavering command.

"No man. It's cool. Like I said, ain't nothing to see." The thief turns and starts to walk away, but Harley is after him in a second.

"I said," Harley says, reaching out and gripping the thief's shoulder so tightly that he can't move. "Show me the phone."

A strangled sound of pain comes from the thief and from the look on his face I can see how hard Harley is gripping him. He hands over the phone and Harley looks at it, without releasing his grip on the thief.

"It sure is interesting that your phone has a photo of my friend here and her father. Because I know that you are not friends with her father."

"Fine, man. Take it. It's yours."

The thief tries to get free of Harley's grip, but Harley doesn't let go.

"Don't ever bother this girl ever again. I find out that you do, and I will pound you into the dirt. Do I make myself clear?"

I stare at Harley, simultaneously grateful that he's just saved my phone and stood up for me, and intensely turned on. My nipples are so hard that they ache and I feel them poking through the thin fabric of my bra. My mind instantly goes to Harley taking my breasts in his large, strong hands and playing with my nipples and claiming the rest of my body.

I blink rapidly as the thief cowers in fear and nod his head. Harley pushes him so hard that he stumbles, but the thief doesn't stop moving and runs away from him.

"I believe this is yours, Justine." Harley's voice and demeanor softens as he turns his attention to me and hands me back my phone.

"Thanks," I say, my hands shaking as I take the phone from Harley. I look at it and put it down on the picnic table and then burst into tears.

"Hey, Justine. It's okay. I'm here. You're safe."

I lean into Harley and he wraps one of his big, muscular arms around me and hugs me tightly to his chest. He lets me cry and I somehow don't feel embarrassed that he's seeing me like this. I feel more angry than anything, but I'm sobbing so hard I can barely catch my breath.

"Justine, it's okay. Shh. You're safe now. I promise."

The rush of fear fades and is quickly replaced by relief. My eyes dry and I look at Harley, once again surprised at the man he is.

"You really are completely not how I expected you to be. Thank you so much for what you did. I know my dad always says to give a thief what he wants, but it's my phone, you know? I just can't give that up."

"I'll take that as a compliment. And your dad is right."

I look up at Harley and raise my eyebrow at him.

"You agree with my dad on something? Didn't I last see you waiting to talk to him? Unless you're an informant, you're a criminal."

The sound of Harley's laughter releases tension in me. I feel safe with him.

"You would be correct on all counts."

"You know, he warned me about you."

"I have no doubt that he did. He also warned me about talking to you." Harley meets my eyes and his gaze is unsettling. His green eyes seem to see deep into me. I know what my dad said, but there's something magnetic about Harley. "The real question is, Justine, what do you think? What do you want?"

I bite my lip and take a deep breath. Can I say the words? Can I really say what I feel?

"I want to misbehave."

HARLEY

Hearing such a sweet girl say that she wants to misbehave with me makes me want to throw her over my shoulder and take her home and fuck her until neither of us can walk. Justine stirs up feelings in me that I've never felt before and it's confusing. She is so clearly a goody good girl and her father is the fucking chief of police. If there's any girl I shouldn't want and I should stay away from, it's Justine.

But no fucking way am I staying away from her. I'm going to make her mine, fuck the consequences with her father.

"Those are dangerous words, Justine. Do you realize how dangerous?" I don't think she is, but there is a voice in my head that says maybe she's teasing me and doesn't really mean it. I run my finger along her jaw and tip her face up to mine, and her pink lips make me hard.

She bites her lip and it's the fucking sexiest thing I've ever seen. She is so close to going over the edge and I can tell that she wants to.

"I know and I do. I'm tired of being the good girl my father expects me to be."

She looks up at me with her dark brown eyes and I'm fucking done for. I haven't even spent an hour with this woman, but there is no way I'm ever letting her go. She may have a prim and proper exterior, but she's as much as admitted she wants to be the sultry bad girl I know she is.

"If you go down this path with me, there's no turning back. I play for keeps."

Justine stares into my eyes and I know I'm on the precipice of something great with her.

"I'm playing for keeps, too."

Hearing Justine say these words unlocks a part of my heart that I've kept carefully closed forever. I pull her face to mine, gently, and tilt her face up and kiss her lips. Kissing her feels like home, like I've found a greater purpose. She reaches behind my head and weaves her fingers through my hair and holds my head tightly, deepening our kiss. I pull her closer to me and growl as her full tits press against my chest. I need to see those tits bouncing above me as she rides my dick.

I freeze at the sound of my phone ringing. Only three people are programmed into my phone so that it will actually ring. Everyone else goes to voicemail.

Pulling away from Justine and ending our kiss is the hardest thing to do. Every atom of my being is screaming to bundle her up in my arms and hold her forever. I want to put her on the back of my bike and show her the world. Show her my world.

Why now? Why does the call have to come now, when I'm spending such a perfect moment with Justine? But it's a call I can't refuse.

"Justine, darling. I have to go."

JUSTINE

"I'm fine, dad." Even I can hear the lie in my voice, but my dad is finally realizing that something serious is going on and I'm just not going to talk about it. He raises his eyebrow at me and goes back to his dinner.

"If you say so, Justine. I know you don't want to talk about it, but I can guess what's on your mind. I can guess *who* is on your mind."

I roll my eyes at my dad. Of course he knows who I'm thinking about. It doesn't take a detective to figure that out.

"Dad, I love you, but I'm not interested in one of your lectures right now. I know you don't like Harley, but there's something special about him. He's different."

"Justine, dammit! You know I can't talk about open cases, but you need to steer the hell away from Harley. He's exactly the kind of man that will take you away from me and ruin your life."

"You have to talk to him like I have. He's helped me. I know that there's something going on below the surface and that's there's something that you're investigating, but he is not a bad man. I know that as well as I know that you're not a bad man, either."

My dad stares at me, not saying anything. I don't often stand up to him, because he taught me to respect his authority. But I know with every fiber of my being, that he's wrong about Harley. It hurts that he had to take a phone call and he just disappeared instantly, but I still know that Harley is good.

"Dad. I can't talk to you right now. I'm going out."

It felt bad talking to my dad like that and leaving him, but I had to get away. I know what he'll say, but my heart is saying something different. I want Harley more than I've ever wanted anyone and it scares me. But it scares me in an exciting way. I've never really dated anybody because my father has sheltered me, but now I understand what my friends talk about when they talk about meeting someone who just makes everything click. I feel that way about Harley, which is so weird because we barely know each other, but I know that there is something special between us. I want to explore that special feeling and see how my life could be with him.

I walk faster, trying to work off my frustration, but it's not working. I know there's something big that Harley is hiding, and I need to know what it is. Only thing is, I don't know how to find him.

Without intending to, I find myself a block away from the park. I don't usually go into the park after dark, because it has a bad reputation. Nightfall is coming, and dad has told me stories of everything that happens there after dark. I'm not foolish enough to court that kind of danger. I haven't told my dad about what happened with the junkie and my phone, and the truth is I'm still a little bit shaken up by that.

I watch other people driving by in their cars, laughing or talking and looking like they belong together. That's what I want. I want to belong with another person and build a life of my own and spread my wings.

It gets dark before I realize it, so I turn around and head for home. I know I'm going to have to talk to dad when I get there, but I put the hard conversation out of my head.

The roar of the motorcycle fills the streets and I instinctively look toward the sound. When I see that it's Harley, my heart leaps and the purest feeling of happiness fills me up. Harley waves at me and I stop walking, watching as he does a U-turn and pulls up next to me.

"Is this a chance meeting or did you track me down?" I tease Harley, stepping close to him and putting my hand on his arm.

"Some of both." Harley takes his helmet off and shakes his head.

I know I should be mad at him that he left me so abruptly, but seeing him and hearing how he tracked me down just erases the frustration I've been feeling.

"I'm sorry about before. It was a very important call and I had to take it."

Harley seems sincere, but it sounds like such a cliché thing to say. I want to believe him, but everything my father says flies back into my mind and I wonder if I should believe my father instead of my heart.

"Harley," I pause, building up the nerve to say what I need to say. "You need to be honest with me about what's going on. You can't be blind to the fact that there are so many red flags about you. I like you, a lot. But you need to tell me what's going on. Show me that I can trust you."

"Damn, Justine. You don't pull any punches, do you?" Harley looks at me, his green eyes looking tender and vulnerable.

He's either the world's greatest actor or something incredibly important is going on. I want to believe him, but it's impossible for me to quiet my dad's voice in my head. As much as I want to, it's hard to step out of my comfort zone and go against what I know.

"Hop on," Harley says, handing me his helmet. "I'll tell you everything, but not here on the street."

Everything in my mind tells me that this is a fantastically bad idea. Getting on the back of a motorcycle with a virtual stranger? My dad would stroke out if he knew that I was even considering it. *Justine, just do it. Follow your heart.*

I fumble with the helmet as I put it on my head and Harley fixes the chinstrap for me. I pull up my skirt a little bit, thankful that it's full and not formfitting, and then get on his bike and wrap my arms around Harley. He's so muscular and big, it's like putting my arm around two men. I let myself lean into his back we roar off down the street, together.

~

"What is this place?" I look around this tiny restaurant and it's deserted. There are just a few tables around and pictures of couples from fifty or sixty years ago. "Are they closing or opening? I can't tell."

"Have a seat, Justine. This place is only open to a few people – it not a regular restaurant." Harley sits down heavily in the chair, and I wonder if it can hold all of his muscles and height. "What has your father told you about me?"

"Nothing, other than to stay away from you."

Harley takes a deep breath and puts both of his hands flat on the table between us. I unexpectedly feel reassured by the gesture, like he's showing me that he's not hiding anything.

"Alright. I'll be honest with you. But I also need you to agree to keep what I tell you between us. Don't tell your father."

"You realize how bad it sounds, don't you?" I lean back in my chair, scared that following my heart was a mistake.

"I do and I'm sorry. Hear me out."

Harley takes off his leather jacket and hangs it over an empty chair. His arms are covered in tattoos, from the back of his hands all the way up to his shoulders and underneath the sleeveless shirt that he's wearing. I bite my lip from how my body responds, because right now his tattoos are the sexiest thing and all I can think about is touching them while he explains what they mean to him.

"I am a criminal. Just not the way your father thinks I am."

HARLEY

I was called into your father's office, the day we met, because he found out that I wired some money to a criminal kingpin in Albania. But what your father doesn't know, is that despite all of the bad things that that man actually does and all of the bad things that I've done in the past, I'm working to fight human trafficking and stop the sexual slavery of women."

Justine stares at me, her lips parted into an O of surprise. She keeps opening and closing her mouth, like she can't decide on what to say. There's an intelligence behind her eyes and I can see her weighing that I'm a man who's done bad things in the past, but who's doing good, now, by working with the bad man who also does good.

"Let me see if I get this straight. You're working with some massive crime lord to stop human trafficking?"

"That is exactly correct, Justine."

"But I don't entirely see what the problem is. You're not doing anything wrong. So what does it matter if you're sending money to Albania?"

"It matters because he's also an arms dealer. And funding that, which is why your father probably thinks I'm doing, is a crime. He's not wrong in thinking that I'm doing something illegal, I'm just not doing what he thinks I am. He thinks I'm funding or buying illegal arms. There are also things that I do to get these women to safety once they're out of Eastern Europe, but I don't think your father understands because he doesn't understand what I'm really doing. These women don't have passports, which means that whichever country they end up in, they're not there legally."

I know my father would say about an illegal immigrant, but this feels different. My heart goes out to these women who have been subjected to such horrific violence. All they can do is run.

"You haven't answered my question. What do you actually *do*?" Justine persists, crossing her arms over her chest and I'm distracted by how fucking sexy this woman is.

"The short answer is I help cover expenses to get women away from traffickers, and then for women who end up in the US, I help them get established in new lives. That means finding them work that's off the books and that won't exploit them, and getting them new identities."

"Oh," Justine says, her body relaxing. "I see what you mean. My dad is hard, but he's also a good man. You should talk to him, explain this."

"Justine, babe." I shake my head. She's so smart and feisty, but also naïve. "That would be a righteously bad idea. He'd throw me in jail."

"No, Harley. Talk to my dad. He's a reasonable man. Maybe if I talk to him, tell him I trust you, then that will help. He deeply believes in justice. You might be surprised. He also deeply believes in the law, but he might be more on your side than you think."

I listen to her and wonder if what she says is true, about her father. When I met with him, he seemed like an absolute by the book kind of cop. The kind of cop who doesn't let even a little thing slide or look the other way when something is illegal but necessary.

"Justine, you need to know this is who I am. I'm not changing. I love you and want you by my side, but you have to understand and accept this about me. With your father," I exhale deeply and shake my head. If I could stay away from this amazing girl, I would, but I can't. She's captured my heart and I can't walk away from her, despite knowing the problems it will cause because of her father.

Justine opens and closes her mouth, her brown eyes boring into me. Waiting for her to say something is worse than being interrogated by her father.

"You… You love me?"

"I do, Justine. I do. It's crazy and I'd understand if you laughed in my face, but you have a magic that I didn't think I would ever find in a woman. You're the only woman for me. Ever."

"I… You're right this is crazy. Ever since that day we met, I felt it. I've felt like I know you, that there was something drawing me to you. I've never felt like this about anyone. I love you, too."

Justine smiles and tears well up in her eyes. I'm immediately on my feet and closing the distance between us, kneeling in front of her and moving as close to her as she'll allow.

My heart is about to explode in my chest. I need Justine more than I've ever needed anyone else in my life. I want to save the world, and I don't want to do it alone.

"Will you stand by my side?"

"Absolutely!" Justine says, getting up from her chair and throwing herself in my arms. I hear the owner, Mo, cheer from the back of the restaurant and look and see him grinning and holding a thumbs up. She gives me a big kiss that melts my reservations about her father. "But now we need to go talk to my dad."

"Harley. I'm going to be honest with you. I'm not crazy about your methods in helping these women, but I admire what you're doing. When I can help you, if I can, I will, but I can't make any promises. Do we have a deal?"

By the time Chief Harwell and I finished talking, he's come around a lot more than I gave him credit for. While Justine patiently waited up in her bedroom, her dad and I sat in his kitchen and had a long talk.

"I can work with that Chief Harwell. Thank you."

"About the other matter." Chief Harwell says, leveling his gaze at me.

I nod, knowing what's on his mind. I look toward the front stairwell and nod my head.

"Your daughter. Justine."

"Yes. My daughter. If you hurt her or put her in danger, know that I will come down on you with the full force of the law and I *will* get the Feds involved. Do we have an understanding?"

"We do, Chief. We do. I love your daughter a great deal and I will do anything, include giving my life, to keep her safe. I swear that on my life." I say all of this, looking straight into Chief Harwell's eyes. While we have some kind of truce between us, I understand exactly how fragile that truce is. I have no doubts that if something happens to Justine, that he will come after me with a raw ferocity that would match my own in his situation.

"Good. Now take care of my daughter and get out of here before I call the police." He laughs at his joke and I laugh with him, extending my hand and shaking his, hard.

"See, Harley. What did I tell you?" Justine looks like a goddess, standing beside my chopper, taking off her helmet and shaking out her hair. Her body jiggles in all the right places and my cock feels like steel. I need to finish the deal and make Justine mine.

"You were right, babe. I honestly didn't believe you, but we did come to some kind of understanding."

I lead Justine through the garage and into my house. It's been a long time since I've had anyone in my home, but this is Justine's home now, too.

"This looks a lot…softer than I would have expected." She pauses in front of an abstract painting that one of the women I've saved sent to me, five years ago.

I explain about the history behind the painting and Justine bites her lip in that sexy way she has, and nods her head.

"We can talk about the artwork and the decor another time," I say, gathering Justine up into my arms and groan with desire as I feel her soft curves and bodacious tits press against my body. I have a need for her to be in my bed and screaming my name, and absolutely nothing and no one is going to interrupt that.

JUSTINE

Harley wraps his arms around me and my heart pounds wildly in my chest. He pulls me close, against his muscular, tattooed body, and waves of emotions overtake me. It doesn't seem possible that I can like a man so much, so fast, and then I feel like I can trust him. I'm not sure if my dad will never fully trust him, but there's a part of me that just doesn't care. I return Harley's hard kiss and wrap my arms around him. I've never felt anything like the passion and power of his kiss.

"I need you in my bed. Now." Harley's voice is deeper, like a growl of his motorcycle.

I bite my lip and look up into his green eyes, and nod my head.

"Yes. I want that, too," I whisper. Just saying these words feels so filthy. "I… I don't know if it matters, but it's…"

"What?" Harley's eyes are alert as he looks at me. "Is there something wrong?"

Harley takes a step back from me, his hands firmly holding my arms.

"No… It's kind of embarrassing, really." I look into Harley's eyes and I realize that I have nothing to be embarrassed about. He's looking at me with such caring and desire, that I know that I can really trust him. "I've never been with a guy before. "

Harley's eyes flare and a smile spreads across his strong mouth.

"You are a daddy's girl, aren't you?" Harley chuckles a little bit, but pulls me close to him again. He kisses me more gently this time, his hands massaging and caressing my body. The more he touches me, the more I know that I want to give myself to him. My body comes to life when he touches me.

"Maybe a little bit. I'll be the first to admit that I've lived a sheltered life, because of my dad."

"Justine, baby. That's not actually a bad thing." Harley sighs heavily and hugs me tightly. "I've… I've seen some terrible things and met women who had terrible things done to them. I sincerely hope your father hasn't seen anything of those things or even read about them. It may have been suffocating to you, but his heart was definitely in the right place. I would protect you with my life, too. You're special, Justine."

My eyes prick with tears as I listen to Harley. I've wanted a man to think that I was special and to love me, and now I've found that with Harley. We've barely met, but it's just so right, like cupid shot his arrow and brought us together.

"Thank you." I lean my head up and kiss his lips, desire burning through my body. His tongue invades my mouth and I go weak as I give myself over to my emotions.

"I will always treat you like a goddess. You deserve nothing less," Harley says, pulling my shirt over my head, then lowering his head and kissing my neck and shoulder. "I will treat you with dignity and love, forever. My men and I will protect you. I love you, Justine. Deeply. I am yours forever."

"Oh, Harley. I love you, too!" I pull at his clothing, even more desperate to feel his skin against mine. "I'm ready for you."

A primal sound escapes from Harley's mouth. We quickly remove our clothes and fall into his bed, our hands stroking and caressing each other. I stare at his tattoos and the scars on his chest, but I close my eyes when I feel his fingers slide between my folds and tease at my clit.

I move my hand down his body until I find his hard shaft, then stroke it and marvel at his length and girth.

"You're so big…" I moan as he plunges two fingers inside of me and strokes a place I didn't know could feel so good. My body takes over and bears down on him, aching for more. "Please, I need you."

Harley moves so that his body is above mine and I gaze up at him, marveling at how powerful and handsome he is. His dark hair falls over his face, but I push it back so that I can watch his eyes as he enters me.

At first, it hurts when he pushes into me, but as I take more and more of him, it feels better than anything I've ever felt before. Pleasure takes over my body and I push my hips up, faster and faster, so I can feel even more pleasure as Harley plunges his cock deeper inside of me.

"Goddamn. You are so tight and you feel so good!" Harley grunts and moans as he works his hips over me. "I need to be deeper inside of you. Get on your stomach."

Frustration tangles inside of me when Harley withdraws from me. I quickly move as he directs and instinctively push my ass in the air for him. I look over my shoulder at him and see him pumping his cock and staring at my ass.

"It's dangerous to wave your ass at me like that. I will claim your ass, but not tonight." Harley's breath is uneven as he puts his hands on my hips and holds me steady as he slides his cock into me again. He pumps fast and each time he hits my g-spot and a different kind of tension builds inside of me and I'm so close to exploding from how good this all feels.

"Oh my God! I never realized sex felt like this!" My breasts are swinging over the bed and the cotton sheets rub against my nipples and makes me feel even wilder. I bounce and wiggle my hips as much as I can, trying to help Harley get deeper inside of me because he feels so perfect. He was made for me and I was made for him, and we are puzzle pieces who finally found each other.

All at once, my body thrashes and a hot sensation builds down there and I can't contain it.

"Right there! Just like that!" I grab at the sheets and work my hips faster and faster. Harley plunges deeper into me, filling me up perfectly and making me his. I cry out and my body explodes and trembles over Harley's cock. He buries himself deep inside of me and I can feel myself grabbing and hugging his cock.

"Fuck!" Harley grabs my hips and pumps in and out of me hard and fierce. My body is so sensitive right now, but it still feels so good to have him inside of me.

"How do you want me? What do you want me to do?" I look over my shoulder at Harley and watch his face as he fucks me. His eyes are wild when they meet mine.

"Turn over and open your mouth."

I quickly do as he says, not sure what he's going to do. I mean, I'll do anything for him. I look up at Harley and pinch my nipples as I open my mouth for him. He moves so that his throbbing cock is right in front of my face. I open my mouth even wider and stick out my tongue so that I can lick him and take him into my mouth.

Harley's groan sounds like a roar and his body shakes and I choke as his come fills my mouth and hits the back of my throat. I keep working my tongue over him as much as I can, but Harley shakes and pulls out of my mouth.

"Fuck. I can't contain myself with you." The look in Harley's eyes as he looks at me is filled with love and happiness. He strokes my hair as I cough and wipe my mouth. I feel a little bit of spit and come fall onto my breasts and I rub his come over my breasts and into my skin.

"I am yours, Harley. Forever."

Harley lays down and wraps his arms around me, throwing one leg over me and holding me close. I couldn't escape him even if I wanted to, and it's not something I could ever do because I love him so deeply.

"You are my woman and I am your old man. Nothing will ever change that you belong to me."

I tremble as I listen to Harley. There is such power and command in his voice, and it excites me. It excites me to know that I have found my match and that I'm pleasing to him. I'm nervous about building a life with him, but only because I'm scared of doing something wrong. I've never been in a serious relationship with someone and it seems so complex. But I'm ready and I know without a shadow of a doubt, that Harley is the one for me. Now and forever.

"I like the sound of that," I say, wiggling my body so that I can wrap my fingers around his cock again. "Can we do that again?"

"Ready for more so soon?" A wicked smile plays on Harley's lips, lust and love making my body shiver in anticipation.

"I love you, Harley. I will always want more with you."

Harley moves his muscular body and lays down on his back. I instinctively move so that I'm straddling his waist, his cock bumping against me. My hands run over his tattooed stomach and chest, and I marvel at all of his tattoos.

"What's this blank spot, here?" I say, running my hands over the top of his chest, by his heart.

"I was saving that for the woman who captured my heart. And that is you, Justine. I'm going to tattoo you on my chest as a symbol of my undying devotion to you."

"You are more than I ever imagined I would find in a man." My heart swells with love for Harley as I push down onto him and take his cock deep inside of me. I rock my hips back and forth slowly, trying to savor how good it feels to have given my virginity to such a powerful man.

"Are you ready for the ride of your life, Justine?" Harley reaches up and pinches one of my nipples and electric pleasure lights up my body. "Fuck, you are so gorgeous."

"Absolutely, Harley. I will ride with you forever."

EPILOGUE

"Thanks, dad. We'll check in when we're home from our trip."

My dad sighs heavily and his eyes crease with concern as he looks at me. We're all standing in the entry way of his house, saying goodbye after having dinner together. Whenever Harley and me are headed out on one of our trips, we stop by to have dinner with my dad.

"I know I can't stop you, but I still wish you wouldn't go. It's dangerous."

"Don't worry Chief Harwell," Harley says, possessively draping his arm around my shoulders and pulling me close to him. "I've got her back. You know that I'll do anything for my Justine. Anything." The way he stresses the word *anything* makes the hair on my arms tingle. The thing is, I know that Harley would do anything to protect me. I haven't been in danger that many times, but I do get scared what might happen when he is protecting me. If he got badly hurt or, heaven forbid, killed, I don't know what I would do. Life without Harley is a scary idea and one I never want to experience.

"That's good, Harley." My dad's voice is stern. He's come around a lot in the last year, but he's still not quite a hundred percent about Harley, despite how much we clearly love each other. My dad appreciates what Harley, and now me, do, but he really doesn't like the methods and I know that as a lawman, it pains him to know that we're breaking the law. It doesn't matter that my dad also wants these women freed and safe, he wants me safe too.

Life with Harley isn't always safe, but I wouldn't have it any other way. We're doing work that needs to be done.

"You have my word, sir. This is just a routine trip, no danger involved." Harley reaches out and puts his hand on my dad's shoulder and my dad tenses at the gesture.

"Dad, really it's okay." I go over to my dad and give him a big hug.

"You're certainly not a little girl anymore," my dad sighs, looking down at me. "Especially not dressed like that. That jacket sure looks out of place with that pretty dress you're wearing."

I grin as I run my hands over my leather jacket. I love this jacket nearly as much as I love Harley. I also love the reason I'm wearing this dress, and it's certainly not one I'd ever share with my dad. Not in a million years!

We finish saying our goodbyes and my dad watches as we get on Harley's bike and ride away. Once we're a couple of miles away and out of suburbia, Harley reaches down to my leg and taps it. It's how we communicate when we're riding. I tap his hand back, to let him know I'm ready, and then he pulls over to the side of a deserted road.

Quickly making sure no one is around, I reach under the loose skirt of my dress and pull my panties down and stuff them in my jacket pocket.

"Ready," I say, grinning. I lay my jacket on the ground and kneel on it as I watch Harley gets off his bike and unbutton his jeans. His thick cock springs out and I lick my lips, so hungry to taste him. He walks slowly over to where I'm kneeling, his hand stroking his cock.

"Let me," I say, reaching out to him. I bite my lip as I feel his hot shaft in my fingers. I lift him up to my mouth and quickly open wide and take him deep into my mouth.

"Oh, fuck. Justine, baby." Harley groans as I begin working my mouth on his thick cock. "I love how you get down to it so fast."

I don't start slow, because I want it. I always want his cock, whether it's in my mouth or in my pussy, or even in my ass. Though in my ass is only for special occasions, because he's so big.

I look up at Harley as I bob my head on his cock, massaging his hot length with my tongue and choking a little when he hits the back of my throat. There's no room for anything else in my mouth, because he fills me up so perfectly. I love giving Harley head and watching how he reacts as I move my mouth. It makes me feel powerful to watch the effect I have on him and to see that vulnerability that appears when his body shakes and his come explodes in thick, white ropes, deep in my mouth and throat. Damn, it makes me feel sexy and turned on!

"Fuck. You are fucking amazing. But I want to come in that sweet snatch of yours."

I pout a little when he pushes my head away and off of his cock, but my pussy is so wet and aching right now, I'd do anything to please Harley. No matter how often we have sex, I always want more and more. He calls me his curvy nympho.

Harley holds out a hand to help me stand up, then we walk back over to his bike and put my jacket in the saddle bag. He gets on first, then helps me to get on, so that we're chest to chest. I cry out when I slide down onto his hard cock, every nerve ending in my body already lit up and ready for the explosion of pleasure that isn't far off.

"You ready?" Harley asks, turning on the engine and giving me a long, probing kiss. I love that he'll kiss me after I've given him head and that he's not afraid of how he tastes. There are no bounds with our sex life and Harley has taught me things I never knew existed.

Like road sex.

"Always, baby. I'm always ready for you." I carefully wrap my legs around his waist, then lock my ankles together. The engine rumbles against my bare ass and I squirm at the pleasure of it. I slide my arms around his torso, his jacket covering me, and nestle my head against his chest.

Harley pulls back onto the freeway and I move my hips as much as I can, which isn't much, rubbing myself against his hard cock buried deep inside of me. Every time he changes lanes and bumps over the reflective markers, I cry out as he hits my clit and g-spot even harder.

There's barely any room for me to move and I have to be careful not to block his view of the road, which makes this a beautifully excruciating exercise in restraint. His cock is buried so deep inside of me, it feels like we are one.

This is a dangerous way to ride, but it's one of the things I love most. I trust Harley completely and the danger of getting caught makes me so wet and horny, that I can't even contain myself.

Harley revs the engine and my body echoes the roar, my first orgasm building from deep inside of me. I lick and suck at Harley's chest, outlining his tattoos with my tongue, especially the one just above his heart.

With the night road almost deserted, Harley changes lanes regularly and when he hits a bump in the road, all of my senses light up and I clench him even tighter and scream into the wind as I come hard all over him. The rumble of the engine beneath my ass pushes my orgasm further and harder, and I rock on Harley's thick cock as I feel his heartbeat race in his chest.

He slows down and pulls over by a stand of trees, and we practically fall off the bike. We get about five feet from the road, then Harley pulls me down onto the ground, spreading my legs wide and plunging his cock back inside of me. We move as one, me crying out as he strokes my spots harder and faster, another orgasm already building inside me, more powerful than the first one.

"You're mine, Justine. Until the end of time, you're mine."

I arch my back and grind down on him, pushing and panting as my orgasm crests, nearly ready to break.

"Always, Harley. You know I'm yours."

An ambulance screams down the highway and masks our screams and groans as we come together, riding each other fast and hard, unrelenting in our passion for each other. Our bodies thrash as we ride out our orgasms, then Harley collapses in my arms. We lock into a passionate kiss as our bodies twitch and shudder from coming, our sexual hunger sated. For now.

This is my life, now. And it's perfect.

This book is part of the CURVY COLLECTIONS series. Are you all caught up?
Get ready to binge!

Want a free book? Join my newsletter and receive *Sweet Temptation*! Find out what happens when a woman with a gluten allergy falls for a bad boy baker!

Subscribers are the first to hear about new releases, sales, and freebies!
https://dl.bookfunnel.com/24haw82y9e

Thank you so much for reading *His Curvy Beauty: Books 1-3*!
If you enjoyed this book, please consider leaving a review on your favorite retailer, Bookbub, or Goodreads! Thank you!!

WHAT SHOULD YOU READ NEXT?

MORE BOOKS FROM LANA LOVE!

Are you ready to fall in love with the heroes of Heartland? Get ready to binge!

Heartland Heroes: The Men of Champ's Gym

Heavyweight He's an up-and-coming boxer with a reputation as a 'love 'em and leave' em' man. She's his coach's curvy little sister…and totally off-limits.

Prizefighter He's a Casanova. She's a curvy nurse with a surprise pregnancy after they shared a hot one-night stand.

Knockout He's a protective boxer who teaches self-defense. She's a curvy woman trying to get away from an abusive ex.

Champion He's stubborn boxing champion. She's a curvy cutie who's his new office assistant and who has a big secret.

Heartland Heroes: The Men of Rebel Autos

Dad Bod Rebel He's a stoic ex-military single dad. She's a sunshine-y teacher who's not scared to fight for the best interests of her students.

A Rebel's Honor He's military vet with a promise to keep. She's the irresistible curvy daughter of his best friend.

A Rebel's Seduction He's a grumpy landlord. She's his curvy tenant and in need of help.

A Rebel's Protection He's a bad boy ladies man with a chip on his shoulder. She's the curvy beauty he thought he was over.

Rebel Boss He's a blue-collar boss and confirmed bachelor. She's a curvy babe who needs his help with an unexpected inheritance.

Heartland Heroes: The Men of King Mountain

Rugged Match He's a reclusive mountain man. She's his best friend's little sister and also the woman who got away.

Rugged Protector He's a confirmed bachelor. She's the curvy woman he protects not once, but twice, and who he gets snowbound with in a cabin with just one bed.

THE KING MOUNTAIN INSTALLMENT OF THE ONGOING HEARTLAND HEROES SERIES BEGINS IN FEBRUARY 2023.

To discover even more books, please visit my website at:

https://loveheartbooks.com/books-by-lana-love/

ABOUT LANA LOVE

Lana Love is a USA Today Bestselling Author of steamy stories about relatable women, and the strong men who will move heaven and earth to capture the heart of the curvy woman they can't live without. Curvy since forever, Lana writes the heroines she never read about or saw in movies when she was growing up.

Lana lives in the Pacific Northwest and is passionate about dancing, travel, chocolate, and cocktails, and writing stories that make her heart race and bring her fantasies to life. She loves a man who loves curves and who knows what to do with them!

For books with relatable women, sinfully hot men, and steam that will melt your e-reader, you've found a new favorite author!

https://www.loveheartbooks.com

You can follow me on social media at:

https://www.goodreads.com/author/show/12219675.Lana_Love

https://www.bookbub.com/profile/lana-love

https://www.facebook.com/groups/746330989530967

Made in the USA
Middletown, DE
30 November 2025